Ring of Stones

Portal to Another World

by

Alexander Lawes

Published under license from Andrews UK

Copyright © Alexander Lawes 2016

First Edition

The author asserts the moral right under the Copyright, Designs and Patents Act 1988 to be identified as the author of this work.

All rights reserved. No part of this publication may be reproduced, stored in a retrieval system or transmitted, in any form or by any means without the prior consent of the author, nor be otherwise circulated in any form of binding or cover other than that which it is published and without a similar condition being imposed on the subsequent publisher.

All characters in this book are fictitious, and any resemblance to actual persons, living or dead, is purely coincidental.

For my wife and children

Grateful acknowledgement is made to
Darin Jewell of The Inspira Group

Chapter 1 – Summer's End

Summer was nearly over, and in a few days it would be time to return to school. The balmy evening air shrouded the city, enveloping it in a dark motherly embrace, shepherding the last commuters home to their families for the weekend.

It was still quite warm, so Harry carried his hoodie, as he meandered aimlessly down the city's streets. He was looking forward to returning to school, which he knew was unusual for a boy of fourteen. The summer holidays had not been as bad as some in the past, but they could so easily have been better.

Harry's parents died when he was young and his grandparents raised him. Since the death of his grandmother it had been simply Harry and his grandfather, who was himself now seriously ill. A nurse came every day, to check he was still alive, as Harry's grandfather would joke. His grandfather drifted in and out of consciousness, and the doctors said it could be any time now.

Harry pretty much fended for himself. He had always been quite a good cook, taught by his grandmother from an early age, and now had little choice but to put his culinary skills to good use. Returning to school would help to distract him from the inevitable, and the worry about what would happen to Harry when his grandfather did finally pass away. Summer had been tedious, mostly made so by the usual taunts from Steve and his gang, which invariably escalated into a scuffle that left Harry with a few bruises or a cut. It was never totally serious; no one was ever properly hurt. Harry knew they were bullies, with complications of their own, which went some way to explaining their rather anti-social behaviour. Not that he sympathised with them, but neither did he particularly care about their personal issues. One day he would let them have it though, he would often tell himself, knowing full well if he did somebody would probably end up badly injured, and it would probably be Harry.

He kicked a stone across the empty road and arrived, as usual, at his local fish and chip shop. Like most it was also a Chinese takeaway, which seemed to upset some of the older people Harry knew, but he wasn't concerned. The fish and chips they sold tasted fine, and he loved prawn crackers, so there was nothing to complain about.

Harry opened the door and went in, the scent of frying causing his stomach to gurgle hungrily. There was a short orderly queue, which suited him as he had yet to decide what he wanted. Sue was working behind the counter, and she looked up and smiled as he joined the back of the queue. Harry liked her; she always gave him slightly larger portions than anyone else when he was alone. Harry wondered if she did the same for all her customers; it seemed like a shrewd sales tactic.

Harry was clever, exceptionally bright for a lad his age, everyone had always told him. His teachers said he would go far, if only he would come out of his shell. They had always said that of Harry, and he thought he knew why. They all knew of the losses he had faced in his life and they assumed because he wasn't especially extraverted, he must be suffering from internal demons, which he refused to talk about. Of course the simple truth was he had always been able to come to terms with whatever life had thrown at him.

Harry had many friends, and was certainly not a loner. He was better than average at most sports, but because he didn't excel at any of them, people would forget, and assume because he was intelligent, he must be rubbish at football. He didn't even wear glasses, but there were those who loved to stereotype all the same - like Steve.

"Yes, Harry, what can I get you?"

Sue's question woke him from his day dreaming. Harry looked about and saw nobody else had come in behind him. "How's your grandfather doing?" she asked gently.

"Not so good," answered Harry. "Please may I just have a small portion of chips today?" he said, quickly changing the subject.

"Of course, coming right up," said Sue with a tight smile. She knew not to pursue the subject. "Your timing is perfect," she said, serving him a large portion of chips from a freshly made batch. She added a scoop of batter scraps in with the chips, folded the paper into a cone with the top open, and passed it to Harry. He paid and with his change came a small bag of prawn crackers.

"Thank you, you're far too generous," said Harry. "You'll never make any money," he laughed.

"Oh, don't you worry about us Harry, we do alright. I'm off to Hong Kong again in a couple of weeks. We don't give out freebies to all our customers you know, only a select few."

Harry thanked her, turned and walked towards the door, which opened before he reached it. Sue's next customer was a girl of about sixteen or seventeen years of age. She was taller than Harry and had short jet black hair, which she failed to tuck behind one ear. Her eyes were a piercing blue, and Harry recognised her immediately. She was two years above him at school, but had joined only a few weeks before the end of the summer term. She had kept herself to herself at school, and spent most of her time in the library with her head down and buried in a book, so all his friends said. Her striking looks had attracted plenty of attention at school, not only from the boys, but she had politely turned them all down. On the couple of occasions she and Harry had passed in the corridor she had fixed him with her bright eyes and beamed at him. He returned the smile, if a little confused by the attention. The second time it happened, of course Steve had to be present, and had been using it as ammunition for his taunting of Harry ever since.

Instead of the school uniform she was wearing the last time Harry had seen her, she was dressed in ripped dark blue jeans, a white t-shirt and a leather jacket. The jacket was black of course and completed her look perfectly, thought Harry. She also wore motorbike boots and carried a helmet, which explained the leather, or certainly was a good excuse for it. Harry grinned to himself, then realised the girl was holding open the door and waiting for him to go out. He hurried through, mumbling his embarrassed thanks as she watched him.

Outside, he paused to admire her 250cc motorbike. It looked street legal but had the sort of knobbly tyres used for dirt tracks. Harry would be the first to admit he didn't know much about bikes, but he was fairly sure someone her age was limited to a smaller engine. For some reason this made him chuckle.

Harry pulled on his hoodie, and ambled away, tucking into his chips and crispy bits of batter, his bag of prawn crackers nestled contentedly in the crook of his arm.

Chapter 2 – Confrontation

The street lamps cast a comforting orange glow over the quiet city evening and Harry felt relatively content, lost as he was in his own day-dreaming. He could see one or two faint stars in the night sky, or were they planets, he could never quite remember? It was one of the drawbacks to living in a built up area, not being able to see the stars. Harry was fairly sure the brighter dot in the sky was the planet Venus. He made a mental note to read up more on astrology, and to extend his walks further out of the city, so he might see what he was reading about. Or was it astronomy? Oh well, it was something else to look up on the internet. He supposed proper space travel to other planets would one day be possible, but not in Harry's lifetime, so instead he allowed his imagination to wander.

"Oi, big head," yelled a voice from behind, startling Harry from his musing.

He knew who it was, and looking over his shoulder, there of course was Steve about twenty metres behind him with four of his cronies, all leering idiotically and clearly looking for trouble. Harry had been enjoying his evening and didn't want it completely ruined, so decided to run for home taking a shortcut down one of the side streets. It would only take him a minute or two as he didn't have far to go, and he would easily beat Steve and his mates.

As soon as he started running, there was a whoop of delight from behind him; the chase was on. Harry smiled in spite of himself, knowing full well how pathetic the whole game was, and there was no real enjoyment in it for him. He turned down the poorly lit side street, the consuming darkness motivating him into a brief sprint, and began putting some distance between him and his pursuers. Enraged by the potential loss of their more energetic prey, the pursuing gang started to shout obscenities at Harry, which he ignored without difficulty, thick skinned as he was.

Steve's voice cut through the others. "So is that feeble old grandfather of yours dead yet?" he barked.

Harry pulled up in an instant. So tonight was going to be the night; he resigned himself to the inevitable fight which was to follow. He waited for them to catch up, facing them with his fists clenched. He had almost reached the far end of the side street, so the lights from the main road now silhouetted him; Harry hoped it made him look bigger.

Steve and his little pack of hounds stopped running and sauntered up to Harry. For an instance Harry wondered if they might be a little intimidated; perhaps it would be like when a cat turns to face the dog that was chasing it, and the dog stops, not knowing what to do next.

Unfortunately, he couldn't have been more wrong. One of the boys ripped Harry's bag of prawn crackers from his hand, causing his cone of chips to fall to the ground. Harry noted the boy was the fattest in the group, and watched as the heavy lad tore open the plastic bag and stuffed his mouth with a handful of crackers, and with an excessive show of generosity distributed the leftovers to his mates. Greedily the selfish mutts devoured the lot, while Steve stood in front of Harry, waiting patiently for some reaction. Harry smirked, thinking his dog analogy wasn't too far out, as the pack wolfed down his food. The boy who had taken the bag returned it empty, jamming it forcefully into the breast pocket of Harry's hoodie, then turned and cackled with his friends.

Harry decided this would be his most opportune moment, and threw a well-aimed left punch at the fat boy's jaw, then jumped at Steve, bowling him to the ground. Harry managed to get in a couple of quick hits, before three pairs of hands dragged him off. They twisted his right arm painfully up behind him, causing him to grimace as he stifled a yelp, which he was determined not to let out. Steve jumped to his feet, and Harry noted a satisfying trickle of blood running from the leader's nose. Harry knew what was coming, but already he felt it had been worth it.

"You are so going to pay for that," Steve promised, as he wiped his nose with the back of his hand, wincing slightly as he did so. Beside him stood the fat boy, who looked no worse for the blow to his chin, but was theatrically rolling up his sleeves. Harry sniggered, the adrenaline pumping round his body giving him courage he didn't know he had.

However, before Steve or his fat friend had a chance to retaliate, a loud noise at the near end of the street startled them all. A motorbike approached, its engine revved once, and fell quiet. The rider propped the bike on its side stand, dismounted and took a few steps towards the disturbed group. Harry thought he probably hadn't appeared quite as threatening as the bike rider. The biker removed her helmet and held it in one hand. A collective sigh of relief greeted the girl as the boys recognised her.

"What do you want?" Steve called out to her. "There's nothing of any interest for you here." He stepped in front of Harry, in a weak attempt to hide what they were doing.

"How do you know what interests me?" she replied. Her voice was soft but measured, conveying a kind of adult maturity, which belied her young age.

"Nothing as far as I know. In fact, the way I hear it, you consider yourself too snooty and important to talk to anyone. So why don't you run along like a good little girly, and we'll pretend we never saw you. That way you won't have to admit you actually communicated with another human being."

Steve hooted at his own joke and looked around at the others who joined him. The girl peered past Steve to look at Harry, before returning her gaze to Steve. "Don't worry," she said to him. "For one thing I don't consider you a human being, and secondly, why would I want to admit to having anything to do with losers like you and your sycophantic followers there? Please credit me with a little taste, won't you."

As they gaped with amazement at her retort, the girl walked the last few steps, closing the space between them.

"Why don't you leave him alone," she said, gesturing towards Harry, "and go home to bed now boys. It must be way past your bedtime and your poor mummies will be worrying about you."

At that they all burst out laughing, including Harry. It was a mistake on his part, as Steve landed an unexpected punch on Harry's stomach, doubling him over as the air rushed from his lungs. The boy holding his arm released him, and Harry dropped to his knees in pain from the surprise blow.

The girl glanced at Harry with alarm, providing Steve with the ideal opening he desired.

"So that's it, is it? You're his girlfriend are you?" he teased, giving Harry a sharp nudge with his knee.

"That's right, I am Harry's girlfriend. I didn't think anybody knew. Oh Harry, you haven't been broadcasting to the world have you? I thought we were keeping it a secret," she replied, much to all their surprise, particularly Harry's.

He stared at the girl incredulously. However did she know his name?

The biggest of the boys stepped towards the girl. "It's alright love. You've given us all something to chuckle at, but now you really must go. We wouldn't want to mess up that pretty little face of yours would we?" He placed a hand on her shoulder, to push her back towards her bike.

The girl reached up and grabbed the boy's hand, turned it over and twisted his wrist forward, bending it and him effortlessly towards the ground as he cried out in agony. As the fat boy moved in, a powerful booted kick met with his belly dropping him to the ground in an instant. Steve received the full force of the helmet pushed into his face, and he clasped both his hands to his already injured nose. Before they even knew what was happening, the last two received similar treatment, leaving the girl the only one standing.

Harry rose to his feet.

"Thanks…," he started to say.

"Anna," the girl completed for him.

A nasally voice mumbled from the ground. "So she's not your girlfriend?" said Steve.

Anna looked down at him contemptuously.

"Moron!" she said, and grinned at Harry. They both laughed, and walked away, leaving Steve and his motley crew behind in the dark alleyway.

Anna pushed along her bike, as Harry carried her helmet. "It's only the next street," he said, explaining where he lived.

"Will they follow us?" asked Anna, gesturing to the pathetic group they had left behind, and who were now watching from the newfound safety of the main street.

"Probably not. They know where I live anyway," said Harry.

"Oh, okay." They walked on in silence.

As they approached Harry's house, he glanced at Anna's attire.

"You know you ought to be wearing leathers all over," he said, regretting it instantly. What must he sound like to her? Anna was at least two years older than him, and he was being pedantic.

To Harry's surprise, Anna chuckled. "You like that kind of thing do you Harry?"

Harry blushed furiously. "No, that's not what I was saying," he spluttered.

"I know you weren't, I'm only teasing," she said. "You were only thinking of my safety. It's rather sweet I suppose."

Harry groaned inwardly as his embarrassment only worsened. Anna realised she was making him even more uncomfortable and apologised. Harry mumbled a quick thanks as they approached the front door of his house, frantically fishing around in his pockets until he found his front door key. He regained his composure as he put the key in the lock.

"Thanks again Anna," he said, handing over her helmet.

"No problem. See you around Harry," she said, then strapped on her helmet, climbed onto her bike and kick-started the engine. With a brief nod to Harry, she pulled smoothly away and rode off into the night.

Harry entered his home, and quietly closed the door behind him. He was glad he hadn't queried the girl about the bike's engine size.

Chapter 3 – Loss

Harry spent much of the next day in mourning; his grandfather had died during the night. The nurse had checked first thing and woke Harry to give him the sad news. They cried together for a while, which benefited them both. Harry had talked to his grandfather a lot in the last few months, and they had become closer than ever.

The nurse left shortly after an ambulance had taken away Harry's grandfather, and not long after, a solicitor who was also a friend of the family visited, advising Harry not to worry about anything; his grandfather had made all the necessary arrangements concerning the funeral. Harry had already decided he wasn't going to go. He felt he had said goodbye, and didn't fancy meeting a load of strangers, all of them pretending they knew and missed his grandfather. All they probably wanted was to discover if they had inherited anything, but the house and small amount of savings were going to Harry. He knew that was a little unfair, but he couldn't be doing with all the fuss. The solicitor advised him someone from social services would be along later to talk to Harry about where he would be moving. That was going to be the toughest part. Harry had schemed and schemed about how he might be able to stay on by himself, but they knew all about him and his grandfather, and there was no escaping the fact he would soon be in a children's home.

Unless he ran away.

The 'nice lady' from social services didn't turn up. Harry had waited in all afternoon, despite being out of bread and milk. Typical, he thought, when he at last left the house to take the long walk to the supermarket. Dusk was falling, and the city lights arched snake-like over him, their glowing cyclops eyes blinking as they turned on one by one. The corner shop had already closed, leaving Harry little choice if he wanted a nice cup of tea. A lump formed in his throat as he thought about it. Living with his grandparents meant he had always had tea, when his friends preferred fizzy drinks. He worried that from then on, any little association would upset him, so pushed the thought from his mind, and took a deep breath.

He had not gone far, when he became aware that a vehicle was pulling up sharply beside him. It was the motorbike from the night before. Harry stopped to see what Anna wanted. She turned off the engine, ignoring the beeping horn of the car which had to swerve round her.

"Hi Harry," she said from inside her helmet.

"You know, you shouldn't stop on the road here. You might upset some of the other road users," said Harry with a cheeky grin.

Anna bumped her bike up onto the pavement. "Happy now?" she asked sarcastically.

"Well, I don't know. I'm not sure the pedestrians are going to be too impressed either," said Harry smiling. It felt good to find something cheerful to talk about, but it was short lived.

Anna laughed, then tensed her lips. "I'm sorry to hear about your grandfather," she said.

"Thanks," said Harry, wondering how Anna knew, or even why she knew. They stood in an uncomfortable silence for a few seconds, before Anna asked, "What's going to happen to you now?"

"I have to go to the shops to get some bread," said Harry, seizing the opportunity to lighten the mood.

Anna giggled. "You know, you ought to be working in comedy, with that sense of humour," she mocked.

Harry smiled back, enjoying Anna's company, and the escape from reality she provided. He wondered how long it would last.

"Fancy a ride," said Anna, unexpectedly offering Harry a spare helmet fortuitously clipped to the back of her bike. The way she spoke it sounded more like a statement than a question.

A hundred thoughts raced through Harry's mind, as he instantly imagined different discussions, where he started by declining on grounds of safety or because he did need to buy that pint of milk. Inevitably all of the fanciful conversations ended the same way.

"Sure, why not," he said, and took the helmet.

Anna helped him to tighten the chinstrap, showed him where to place his feet on the pegs, and he climbed on behind her.

"Hold on tightly," she commanded, and kicked the bike into action. Harry grabbed round her waist, as Anna opened the throttle, dropped the clutch and they bounced onto the road.

Harry had never ridden on a motorbike before, but in an instant he loved it. They were still in the city, so were not going too fast, but it felt exhilarating all the same. The road seemed so much wider than when he was in a car, and they weaved effortlessly around any vehicles they came up behind. The warm summer city air whistled past his helmet, and their reflection rippled and flowed across the windows as they passed by houses and shops. The emotions of the day were, for the moment, forgotten and Harry realised his cheeks were hurting a little from the huge grin hidden beneath his helmet.

He felt free.

They slowed to a stop at a set of traffic lights, and waited impatiently for the amber light. Anna shifted her weight round slightly and yelled at Harry over the noise of the engine. "Lean with me as we go into the bends. Don't fight it."

"Okay," Harry called back.

The lights changed and they pulled away promptly. They swept round a couple of large roundabouts, nimbly overtaking the clumsy cars, and followed the long straight radial road to the edge of the city with the promise of the open road beckoning them ever onwards. Harry turned his head carefully, so he could see the road behind them out of the corner of his eye. It stretched away, the bright hub of the city-centre radiating light into the night sky, and above the roofs of the buildings the cathedral spire, majestically lit up by its white spotlights, watched over the city.

They turned a corner and the urban lights vanished. Harry looked forward again, peering around Anna's helmet at the road ahead, illuminated by the bike's single headlamp. Anna shifted up through the gears, leaving the city speed limit behind them, as they slipped away into the comforting darkness of the surrounding countryside.

Chapter 4 – Ring of Stones

Half an hour or so later they pulled off the road onto a narrow dirt track, coming to a stop a hundred yards further on at the edge of a small copse. They dismounted and Anna pushed the motorbike behind a bush, where she laid it on the ground and placed their helmets beside it.

"Where are we?" whispered Harry.

Bright moonbeams squeezed their way between the clouds and their light filtered softly through the leaves of the trees. Anna put a single finger to her lips, beckoned to Harry, and they returned to the track. In silence they followed the trail through the trees to its end, where they crouched down beside some low lying bushes. In front of them was a large grass field and in the middle was a ring of large standing stones, some capped with lintels. Harry knew the prehistoric site well, having visited several times before on school trips. While it was always nice to get away from school, it was actually quite boring, so he wondered why Anna had brought him here.

A momentary break in the clouds revealed the full splendour of the full moon. Harry used the light to give Anna an enquiring look. She grinned at him, moved back a few feet into the wood and stood up. Harry followed tentatively, as the shy moon hid itself away once more.

"Have you ever touched the stones?" whispered Anna.

"No, you're not allowed to, and they're fenced off anyway."

They skipped over the second fence, which was nothing more than a single low wire, and within a few seconds they had dropped flat on the floor behind one of the giant stones of the outer ring. As the moon came out once again, they quickly regained their breath, and Harry noted the sweet smell of freshly mown grass from the area around the stones.

"You're quite fit Harry," said Anna. Despite being in the shadows of the stones, there was enough light for them to see one another quite easily.

"Thanks, that was fun," said Harry, although he was nervous about how exposed they might be, should the guard look in their direction.

"I'm glad you thought so, but that was nothing."

Anna reached into an inside pocket of her jacket and produced a small device, which looked not unlike a mobile phone. Harry watched her inquisitively. He had never bothered with a mobile phone of his own, but knew he would need to get one eventually.

Anna flipped open a panel, pressed a couple of buttons, closed it and returned the device to her pocket.

"Time to go," she said, standing up abruptly, her back to the stone. Harry joined her, and could now see the headlights of the cars passing by on the main road only a couple of hundred yards away.

"Now, we are going to walk straight forward into the middle of the inner ring," explained Anna.

"Okay," said Harry, wondering if this was probably about the worst idea Anna had had yet; surely somebody would see them.

"And one more thing Harry. You'll have to hold my hand. It's only for a few seconds, so it won't mean we're engaged to be married or anything."

"Okay," said Harry again, laughing out loud. He clamped his hand to his mouth, his eyes wide with shock at his outburst.

"Definitely time to go," said Anna, grabbing Harry's hand and pulling him forwards.

As they passed into the inner ring of stones, it felt to Harry like they had entered a building with subdued lighting. The evening air became still and the noise of the traffic on the road disappeared completely. The ground hardened under foot and it seemed as if they were inside a room, yet Harry could see the dark countryside all around him. Strangest of all though was the sight of an elderly man reading a local newspaper and sitting behind what looked like an airport check in desk in front of them. The man looked up and smiled when he saw them.

"Hello Anna," he said, "back from your holiday already?"

Chapter 5 – Checking In

"Hi George, how are you? You're looking as well as ever I see," replied Anna.

Confused though Harry was, he did not miss the fact Anna had not answered the man's question.

"It's always a pleasure to see you Anna," said George, coming to his feet. "You're always so charming. If only all the travellers that passed my way were the same." He turned to Harry, who immediately felt guilty, but didn't know why. "And who is your new friend?" asked George without taking his eyes off Harry. George appeared to be quite elderly, slightly stooped as he was, with a few white whiskers about his chin, which he must have missed while shaving on more than one occasion. His eyes however displayed a youthful exuberance, hinting at a keen mind concealed behind his aged visage.

"George, please allow me to introduce Harry. He's going to be coming with me," said Anna pointedly.

"Hello," said Harry, stepping forward and shaking the old man by the hand.

"A pleasure to meet you young man," acknowledged George without any hint of irony. "I'm quite sure if you are a friend of Anna's, we will be friends as well."

"Thank you, I'd like that," said Harry. He was quickly warming to the elderly gentleman.

George turned his attention back to Anna. "Polite though you are Anna I hope you've been behaving yourself, hmmm?"

Anna feigned shocked surprise. "How could you suggest such a thing? When have I ever given you reason to think otherwise?"

George looked at Harry and winked, nodding in Anna's direction. "So this young beauty hasn't been breaking too many hearts?"

"No, not too many," answered Harry.

Anna blushed.

Harry continued, "Although there was this one boy called Steve…"

"Right, that's enough from you two," said Anna sternly, metaphorically stamping her foot. "I am standing right here you know."

"I love it when you get angry Anna," said the old man, chuckling at her.

"You haven't seen me angry," she replied, her eyes narrowing menacingly.

"Steve has," chipped in Harry. He was enjoying himself.

Anna fixed him with a piercing look. "Do you want to come with me or not?"

"Yes, of course, sorry," said Harry sheepishly.

"Ah, young love," sighed George.

"No, we're only friends. We only met a couple of days ago."

"Oh really," said George, becoming quite serious.

Anna jumped in quickly. "What Harry means is we have got to know one another better in the last few weeks, but have been friends for several months now."

Anna's eyes bored into Harry's. He had clearly made some sort of mistake, and wished he had kept quiet.

"Yes, of course," he said as nonchalantly as possible.

George visibly relaxed. "Oh good, that's all right then."

He sat down and keyed in some details at his terminal.

"Right, here we are. Your gate transponder is showing up quite clearly, but naturally it would be, otherwise you wouldn't have passed through the hub's shield." He smiled up at them. "I've booked you in Anna, as you plus one companion. You know you can take two with you now don't you?"

"Yes, thanks George, but it's just the one today thank you."

Harry didn't much understand what they were discussing, but he was beginning to get quite excited about what was in store for him. He did not want to let his imagination get the better of him, but he had already had to accept the impossible when they entered the ring of stones. He looked around again at the room they were in, and at the standing stones and the world beyond. All were faintly visible to him in the darkness, but the lights of the cars on the road were plain to see, and he could even see the torchlight of the security guard as he started another circuit of the stones.

"It'll take a few minutes to book your slot," said George, glancing up. He looked at Harry. "Of course, this is your first time. Anna, why don't you show our young friend around."

Anna huffed. "He's joking of course. But I will explain a little."

She cast her arm around her. "This is the hub. As you undoubtedly have guessed already, we are invisible to the outside world. We passed through the barrier and inside is projected a sort of physical augmented reality, which only we can see. My transponder communicates with the hub, allowing us in where we can see George but not be seen by the outside world."

She sounded most knowledgeable to Harry and he was suitably impressed.

Anna laughed. "To be honest, I don't really know what I'm talking about. I vaguely recall there's a bit more about harmonics or something, but I'm only repeating what I've been told. George, do you know how all this works?"

"Haven't a clue!" he said without looking up from the terminal. "I just work here."

Harry wasn't so sure, feeling the old man knew more than he was letting on.

Anna continued, "I do know if anybody came through the stones now, like that security man, we would need to keep out of his way. He might walk right into us, even though he wouldn't be able to see us, and would probably sense something like somebody had walked over his grave, as you might say."

"The summer solstice is a nightmare," added George wearily. As if to prove his point, George and his desk swung in an arc through ninety degrees, catching Harry quite by surprise.

Anna laughed. "Those druids certainly keep you on your toes, don't they George."

"They're a blinking nuisance," he said frowning, before quickly brightening up. "Okay, we're ready. I'm afraid it's merely the formality now Anna my dear."

"No problem, I'm used to it," she replied, standing in front of him, and placing her right hand on a square yellow light that had appeared on the desk's surface.

George looked at her seriously. "Do you Anna, have the authority to travel with this companion?

"Yes, I do," she replied confidently.

Perhaps a little too self-assuredly Harry thought to himself, but they had nothing to fear as the square quickly changed to green. Harry assumed turning to red would have not been a good result.

"Perfect, it's as simple as that," said George. "You'll be wanting door number three, just behind you." He nodded towards the stones where they had entered.

"The same way we came in," stated Harry.

"Sort of," said Anna, as a large yellow number three appeared on the floor in front of the stone doorway, bathed in the same yellow light. "Thanks George, see you soon," she said and held out her hand for Harry to take hold.

"Yes, thank you George. Nice to have met you," added Harry.

"So long kids, have a great time," replied the old man.

Harry reached for Anna's hand and they crossed over the number three and walked through the portal.

Chapter 6 – Arrivals

Harry was all prepared for something strange to happen, but was a little surprised when he felt no more than a slight twinge in his stomach. What startled him more, however, was the sudden sight of dozens of people milling around him. He didn't have time to take in much as Anna pulled him onwards.

"We have to keep moving Harry," she said under her breath. "Don't cause a scene, and if anyone talks to you, don't say a word, just smile sweetly," she said, dropping his hand as he fell in beside her.

About two dozen yellow gateways encircled the dispersal area, which they marched quickly across. Curious looking people in various outfits were streaming purposefully in and out of them. Some were greeting friends or relatives by long embraces or by clasping one another's arms, similar to a handshake but reaching past the hand to the lower arm. Anna and Harry skirted a circle of check-in desks in the centre, which looked much like George's single desk back in the hub. Clearly this was a similar setup to the one in the ring of stones, but was on a far larger scale. They were inside an impressive hall which Harry considered to be much like a departure lounge at an airport. Unlike George's hub however, this appeared to be purpose built and not hidden away secretively where nobody could stumble upon it accidentally.

One of the people behind the desks waved and called out to Anna as they passed by. The woman spoke in a peculiar language Harry could neither understand nor guess at its place of origin. Anna responded briefly in English and smiled as she walked on. Harry followed closely behind, unable to take in much although he thought he detected a faint smell of freshly baked bread. He assumed it was artificial and produced to present an inviting scent to new arrivals.

They hurried towards an exit doorway and left the hall without further incident. A long corridor stretched ahead of them with rooms off to the sides. As they passed them Harry perceived what looked like storage lockers filled the rooms. On entering the fourth room on the left, this proved to be true. Anna took out her gate transponder and held it up to the door of a locker, which clicked open. Inside were various different looking outfits, some of which were similar to the clothes Harry had seen the other people wearing. Anna reached into the locker and removed a device, which looked like a small version of her transponder, which she gave to Harry.

"Put this in your pocket," she said. Harry did as instructed and Anna breathed a visible sigh of relief.

"Good, now you will be able to understand what people are saying to you, and more importantly, they will understand you."

"It's a translator," said Harry.

"That's right. Without it, to anybody else you'll sound like a babbling fish or something," explained Anna, giggling. She had definitely relaxed now thought Harry.

"Do we have to change clothes as well?" asked Harry, looking inside the locker.

"No, there's no need. All sorts come and go on this planet. Nobody will give us a second look here."

"So we're no longer on Earth?"

"No Harry," replied Anna slowly. "We are most definitely no longer on Earth."

"Thought not," said Harry.

"By the way, well done on your first space jump, Harry. Most people are sick the first time, and some never really get used to it," said Anna.

"Oh yeah, no problem, I'm always doing stuff like that, you know, back on Earth, where I come from."

Anna grinned.

"Speaking of which," continued Harry. "Where are you from, and where are we?"

"All in good time Harry. Remember, not too many questions please," Anna reminded him. "Enjoy yourself, and try to take in and learn as much as you can by listening and looking about. You may find you won't need to ask."

Harry chuckled; this was far more of an adventure than he had been expecting, when they set off on Anna's motorbike only a couple of hours earlier.

Anna led the way out of the locker room and back into the corridor. Harry followed her towards the exit at the far end, over which there was a sign in weird but pretty looking characters. It was not unlike Arabic writing he had seen on television. Although the script was alien to him at first, the words distorted, reformed themselves and Harry was able to read them; all part of the universal translator he assumed. The sign read, 'Welcome to Tamarisk.' At least Harry now knew the name of the planet, even if he didn't know where in the Universe they were.

They blinked their eyes as they stepped out into the daylight. Harry saw at once there were two suns in the sky. One was low down on the horizon and appeared to be setting in a huge glorious red glow. The chasing sun, which was significantly smaller, was a little higher and had more of an orange hue. Together they cast a calm subdued haze over the city spread out before Harry and Anna.

Clearly the builders had deliberately sited the terminal on top of a hill so as to afford visitors and returning travellers with a spectacular sight. The predominantly reddish green city sprawled with vegetation, as gardens and trees surrounded every construction. In general, the buildings were only a couple of stories high, albeit adorned with garden roofs, which overflowed and draped down the sides, intertwining with plants climbing up from the ground. Peppering the landscape, huge skyscrapers, or cloudscrapers as Anna referred to them, rose elegantly from the centres of large parks, and the aptly named glass coated towers reached far into the clouds.

The city stretched in all directions as far as Harry's eye could see. He noted the roads, bordered by all manner of unusual plants, were swarming with large round bubble-like cars, some of which linked together and moved in trains. Occasionally one would split out from the middle to take a different route, and the others would quickly close the gap.

Harry and Anna walked a short distance down the side of the terminal and away from the viewpoint, deliberately unspoilt by the usual busy pick up bays found outside terminals on Earth. They approached a large pool of bubble cars, where travellers were either arriving or selecting a vehicle for their onward journeys. Anna selected one such car and opened a gull-wing door for Harry to enter.

"All aboard who wish to travel in style," said Anna, sweeping her arm towards the bubble car's interior.

"I'm quite disappointed actually," Harry said cheekily, stepping into the car, and taking one of the six spacious inwards-facing seats.

"Well, I am terribly sorry we don't measure up to your expectations," Anna replied, feigning indignation. "Perhaps sir would prefer a more suitable planet next time, maybe one with flying cars instead?" Anna climbed in and sat down opposite Harry, as the door closed automatically behind her.

"Yes, that would be quite acceptable, thank you," Harry replied serenely.

Anna tapped onto a small screen set in the armrest of her seat, fixing Harry with a deliberate stare.

"Okay – next time."

Harry's mouth dropped open, and Anna smirked smugly.

Chapter 7 – Sky High

The bubble car moved slowly out of its parking bay and hooked up with half a dozen others, which snaked their way through the car pool and merged onto a road that channelled them down the hill. They accelerated surprisingly quickly, but not so fast as to be uncomfortable. All the same, Harry looked around for a seatbelt.

"The cars don't need them," Anna reassured him, "they never crash."

She showed him how to operate his seat, so he could rotate to face outwards, and watch the world as it flashed past. They reached the bottom of the hill, where they broke away from their little train, turned through a long bend and joined a new road. Harry reclined his seat, as they quickly caught up with a long train of about twenty cars, and gazed with wonder at the now deep orange tinted city speeding past his window.

The journey was soon over, as the car broke away from the main route, and turned towards the nearest cloudscraper. Harry noted several passengers in the adjacent cars staring after them, and wondered if it was unusual to see people going the way they were taking.

The road sloped down, taking them beneath the beautiful park that surrounded the cloudscraper, and through a long tunnel, which ended in a small car park. There were only six cars parked up, and as they arrived, an empty bubble car pulled away automatically to allow them in.

Leaving the car behind them, Anna led the way to one of two glass lifts. Once inside, she pressed the two numbers required to take them up, and the lift rose effortlessly, passing briefly through the ground above the car park, and sliding up the outside of the building. The speed was much like the bubble car, fast and smooth, and definitely comfortable.

"What did you think of the car ride?" asked Anna.

"To be honest I think I preferred the motorbike," Harry replied.

"Me too," Anna agreed readily.

The lift quickly came to rest about two thirds of the way up the cloudscraper, and the door opened silently, leaving Harry little time to appreciate the wonderful view afforded by the transparent lift. They followed a sparse dimly lit corridor, passing many doors and other hallways, until they arrived at a door, which looked no different to any of the others. Anna offered up her transponder, as she had with the locker, and the door clicked open.

"Welcome to one of my homes," said Anna, pushing open the door for Harry to enter.

"One of your homes?" asked Harry, "and exactly how many homes do you have?"

"Several as it happens, but no more than two on any one planet of course. Some might consider that excessive!"

Harry laughed and walked into the apartment, immediately crossing the hallway into the first room and gazed out of the full length window at the stunning view meeting his eyes. They were about a mile high, and even the hill where they had arrived a short while ago looked tiny. Anna joined him at the window.

"Not bad eh?" she said.

Harry drew in a deep breath. "That's the understatement of the year," he replied.

He looked to the horizon, where the city still didn't come to an end.

Anna explained. "The whole country is pretty much one great big city. You would have to travel over three hundred miles to reach what you would consider real countryside. This is a wonderful place in a developed sort of way, but give me Earth any day."

"But if there aren't any fields, where does your food come from?"

"Why, are you feeling hungry?"

"Starving!"

"Wait here and I shall see what delicacies I can rustle up in the kitchen."

Harry returned to admiring the view. He noted the land was almost totally flat, with only the cloudscrapers and the one hill for the arrivals terminal rising above the other buildings.

"There's only one hill," he called out, looking over his shoulder, and for the first time properly taking in the room he was in. It was small with only one sofa-like piece of furniture and a table beside it. There were no pictures on any of the walls.

Anna's head peered round one of two doorways. "It's artificial," she explained, "purely to give visitors an amazing sight on their arrival. It's the only view most people get to see. Few can afford a place like this. I'm lucky," adding quietly, "my parents left it to me." Her head bobbed back into the kitchen.

"Oh," Harry said softly, shocked by her solemn revelation.

He settled on the sofa, which conveniently faced the window. The small orange sun was dropping quickly below the horizon, and pale blue lights all across the city were blinking on. "Why would anyone want a television with a view like this?" he murmured to himself.

Anna returned, sat down beside him, and handed over a glass of water and a colourful bag about the size of a large crisp packet.

"Dinner is served," she said with an elaborate flourish.

Harry opened the bag tentatively, and looked at the contents. Inside was a selection of oddly shaped objects of various sizes and colours. He read the side of the packet, which merely said, Selection Pack.

"Well don't wait for me, you tuck in," Anna said encouragingly, with a gleeful glint in her eye.

Somewhat dubiously, Harry picked out a small piece and put it in his mouth. The sudden overwhelming flavour assaulting his senses shocked him. It was quite pleasant, but he was unable to associate the flavour with anything on Earth. The texture was somewhat chewy, but easy to eat. Harry tried another, this time choosing a larger piece, and a similar but subtly different surge of flavours met his palate.

"Pretty good," he said, helping himself to some more.

"Well you can live on it," said Anna, "but it tastes like…"

A voice, which seemed to Harry like it came from the walls, fortunately interrupted her. A man's head illuminated the entire wall next to the window, as he proceeded to read the news.

"Would you like to watch this?" asked Anna. "It's timed to come on now if I'm at home."

"Is it as boring as the news on Earth?"

"Worse if anything," groaned Anna.

"I think I shall pass thank you," said Harry, stretching his arms and yawning. "I'm quite tired actually."

"In which case, I shall show you to your room," said Anna, pressing on the armrest of the sofa, which turned off the picture on the wall, and replaced it with subtle colours slowly drifting around and blending together.

Anna showed Harry to a spare room, which was one of two other rooms off the hallway. The bedroom was quite small with no windows, but it was functional, with its own bathroom. Anna opened a section of wardrobe, and explained it would clean any clothes placed in it overnight.

"I'll leave you to figure out the rest," she said. "I hope you sleep well. It's a thirty hour day on this world, so you get ten hours to sleep at night."

"I'm sure that won't be an issue. It's been an amazing day. I'm still struggling to take it all in."

"Well, you wait 'til you try the toilet! Good night."

Chapter 8 – "Shopping" Trip

"Wow, I see what you mean," said Harry the following morning. "That flush is quite something."

Anna grinned at Harry. "Ready for some breakfast?" she asked.

"Definitely, I slept really well. Yesterday seems like worlds away."

Harry paused, and Anna raised her eyebrows. He realised what he had said.

"Okay, don't say anything," he cringed.

"I wasn't going to," said Anna, "hungry?"

Breakfast consisted of another packet of food, the contents of which were much like dinner the night before, but less sweet, and with a more crunchy texture. A glass of hot lemon water accompanied the dried food.

"I thought we might go out today," said Anna. "I'll show you around."

"Great," said Harry between mouthfuls of his breakfast-in-a-bag.

"If anybody asks, we'll say you're my distant cousin from Earth who has come to stay following a bereavement."

"Good idea, the best lies are always those closest to the truth."

"Indeed they are Harry. I think there's more to you than meets the eye, but then, I knew that already."

They finished their breakfast, quickly tidied the flat, and left by the only door, Anna pulling it shut behind them. They took the lift down, Harry marvelling once again at both the view and the speed of their descent, and briefly catching a glimpse of the second sun following the first up from the horizon. This time however, they didn't stop at the car park, but went down another level, where the door opened, and they exited the lift.

"Does it go any further?" Harry asked, looking back as the door closed and the lift silently returned to collect new passengers.

"Yes, it goes down one more level to the return line," replied Anna. "This is where we catch the tube, as you would say."

A short corridor led them out into a large space, much like one of London's underground stations. All along the walls down both sides of the single track were corridors leading to more lifts to the building above, and a wide walkway arched up and over the track, connecting the two platforms. Dozens of business-like people joined them and several waved or greeted Anna amicably. Harry assumed they were her neighbours from the cloudscraper above.

They didn't have long to wait. A rush of air preceded the sleek white polished underground train, which eased quietly into the station. The doors opened, and as nobody exited, the waiting passengers all embarked from both platforms.

Harry and Anna boarded the carriage in front of them.

"We use the underground for longer journeys," explained Anna, as they sat down in the large forward facing seats.

"Where are we going?" said Harry, adding quickly, "if I'm allowed to ask."

"Into town of course," answered Anna.

"Of course," said Harry. He sensed that was all he was going to get out of the secretive girl for now.

The journey lasted about a quarter of an hour, travelling at a speed Harry could only guess at, making one stop along the way, where more commuters joined them. The windows turned black shortly after their rapid acceleration from the station, preventing the passengers from seeing the tunnel walls, which Harry assumed would not have been a pleasant sensation due to their great speed.

They chatted amiably, mostly about Earth and school until the train arrived at a second station. The windows cleared and Harry saw hundreds of people waiting to get on. Anna and Harry exited with a couple of other passengers, whilst the majority remained on board. Once the disembarking passengers were clear of the train, the mass of waiting commuters surged forward and boarded, destined Anna explained, for the city. Since the whole country was one great sprawling metropolis, Harry was unsure of the distinction.

"Right, today is going to be all about fun," said Anna as they caught a lift to the surface.

"And tomorrow?" asked Harry.

"Tomorrow we get serious," came the reply.

"Oh," said Harry.

The lift doors opened on to what looked to Harry to be not unlike an Earth shopping mall.

Anna explained. "These places didn't used to exist on this world. There was no need. People can see and order whatever they like from home on our version of the internet and have it delivered to their doors. But as more and more travellers returned from Earth, with amazing stories about huge shopping complexes, where customers could actually touch the things they wanted to buy, well this is the result. We now have our own malls, not that you can purchase anything. We still have to go home to place an order, but maybe in time we'll be able to buy from shops like we do on Earth."

They walked on past several stores, where window shoppers were excitedly touching and stroking the goods on display. Harry found it a little disturbing.

"Isn't that a bit like us, but going backwards?" he said, furrowing his brow. "I mean, we used to buy from high street shops, but now many people do all their shopping on-line."

"Ironic, isn't it?" said Anna.

At the far end of the mall, they took the escalator up to the next floor. Harry observed that the escalator was almost identical to those on Earth, only it was of course silent in its operation and completely smooth.

"They're talking about adding bumps and sound effects, to make them more authentic." Anna giggled.

"You're not serious?"

"Unfortunately I am. Simply because we're on a different planet light years away from Earth doesn't mean there aren't any people capable of coming up with bonkers ideas."

They walked along the length of the mall turning left at the end where it continued in an L shape. Harry looked at the items in the store windows as they passed. Many of the things were much like the few belongings and furnishings he had seen in Anna's flat; he saw the cleaning wardrobe in one store and a wall sized screen in another. Harry also noticed that, as per the day before, the people in general looked much like anyone on Earth. Sometimes their skin colour was a little different, or their physique was less Earth-like. Their clothes however varied considerably. Those people with slightly smaller heads and a pinkish tinge to their complexion generally wore tight figure-hugging garments. Harry quietly asked Anna if they were the indigenous race on the planet, as they appeared to be the most numerous.

Anna replied that they were, and Harry enquired how it was all peoples were humanoid in shape. They all had one head, two arms, and two legs and as far as he could see, eight fingers, two thumbs and he assumed ten toes.

"I wondered if you might ask, and you're quite right. It would seem that all over the galaxy, the dominant intelligent species capable of discovering interstellar travel is always humanoid. Isn't it amazing we've all evolved the same way, no matter which planet we're from?"

Harry agreed, it was mind-boggling, he thought.

"Of course," added Anna. "Maybe it's not by chance, but by design."

"You mean some all-powerful being created us all that way?"

"Maybe, but I guess that's up to each of us to decide for ourselves."

They both fell silent for a while, and reaching the end of the mall, they took the down escalator.

Chapter 9 – Board Now

"Are you any good at skateboarding?" asked Anna.

They had left the mall and were following a winding path through beautiful gardens filled with bright flowers exuding delicate odours, which led towards a rather small and drab looking building.

"Not really, I prefer street surfing," replied Harry. "Oh, and I once tried snowboarding on a school skiing trip to France. That was great fun."

"In which case, you are going to love this."

They entered the mundane looking building through a side door, the inside of which was similar to the locker room at the Terminal. Anna opened one of the many lockers using her transponder and reached inside.

"Here you go."

Anna tossed over a thick board, which resembled a skateboard without any wheels, fitted with a pair of foot bindings on top.

"This can't be what I think it is," said Harry, examining the board in his hands.

"That depends on what you're thinking."

"It's a hover board, right?"

"Indeed it is," Anna confirmed to Harry's great delight. "No flying cars here, but this is the next best thing. Let's go out and give it a go."

"And you can go anywhere on it?"

"No, what you've described is an anti-gravity board, but you won't be riding one of those."

"Why not?"

"For two reasons actually. One – they don't exist. And two – nobody has succeeded yet in taming that particular law of physics, so I don't think we'll be seeing anti-gravity boards anytime soon."

"So how does the hoverboard work clever-clogs?"

"By following the dotted blue lines, obviously. Buried in the ground are cables creating a strong electromagnetic field, which magnets in the boards use to hover."

"Won't it give me cancer or something?"

"There is a slight risk, but don't worry. If you do, we'll get it zapped."

"You mean on this world there's a cure for cancer. It could save millions back on Earth."

"I know, it's one of the most difficult things to come to terms with. If it's any consolation I think Earth will solve the whole cancer business pretty soon."

"Why does the board have straps?" asked Harry.

"Because we'll be going pretty fast." Anna tossed him a helmet. "You'll need this as well."

Carrying their boards and helmets, they exited the building via double doors on the opposite side of the room. Outside were two boys strapping on their own boards. They were sitting on the ground next to a blue dotted line, and nudged one another when they saw Anna, who pretended not to notice. Harry watched as they stood up, and one after the other they jumped towards the line. The invisible field beneath them cushioned the boards, so they floated a couple of inches above the ground. The first boy moved slowly forward and angling his board towards the blue markings, he and the board rose up until he was a foot off the ground and was rapidly picking up speed. His friend followed suit, and they banked round a corner and were gone.

As usual, Anna explained. "Picture it like a long invisible mound. The further you are from the centreline the lower and slower you will travel. If you want to go faster, move towards the midpoint, and as you rise up, that's what will happen. If you want to go even faster, lean forward, and when you want to slow down or stop, lean back and angle towards the side of the mound. Don't lean forward when you're low down though, as you're liable to dig the nose into the earth and the ground here isn't as forgiving as snow."

"What about turning?" asked Harry.

"Easy, just lean into it. Don't worry, you'll get the hang of it in no time at all," Anna reassured him, as they put on their helmets, tightening them with a small knob on the side.

"But isn't there a risk of flying off, if I take a corner too quickly?" asked Harry, a little nervously.

"No, stop worrying. The field grips you in place. The higher up you are, the closer you are to the middle of the field, and the more secure you'll be. It's all about confidence. Trust me."

She stepped onto her board, bent down and tightened the bindings, securing her feet. With a light hop, Anna landed neatly on the edge of the invisible field, where she hovered, leaning back slightly to prevent the board from moving forwards.

Harry sat on the ground forward of Anna, and clipped himself onto the board. He stood up confidently, and jumped towards the blue line on the ground in front of him. He felt the board bounce lightly on the electromagnetic field, and bent his knees to steady himself. The board moved slowly forward and he could feel a subtle vibration and hear a soft whirring noise emanating beneath him. Harry wobbled and lost his balance, sitting heavily back down on the ground.

"You need to get up a bit of speed quite quickly," said Anna. "It's tricky to balance if you go slowly." She turned steeply up the unseen field, spun on the top, and returned stylishly to her start position. "Until you've had a bit of practice, that is."

Harry chuckled at her display of showing off. He stood up again, hopped forward, and immediately turned the board toward the centre line. He rose smartly to the top of the field, and aimed positively for the first bend. Anna whooped a cry of delight, and followed closely behind.

They glided through the first corner, the invisible force beneath their feet grasping them tightly as they banked round. There followed a smooth series of bends, where the hidden camber flicked their boards from left to right and back again as they negotiated the twists and turns of the course. They accelerated out of the last bend onto a long straight, which passed by the back of a row of single story buildings. Harry felt exhilarated; the sensation of hovering above the ground and travelling at speed without fear of crashing was truly unlike anything he had ever experienced.

Abruptly Anna yelled out a warning. Approaching them from the opposite direction were the two lads who had left a few minutes earlier.

"Move to the left hand side," Anna called out to Harry, who did as instructed, noting to his relief that the oncoming boarders had also moved to their left.

The two groups passed one another slowly and safely. Harry realised they were all riding regular, with their left foot forward, so as they passed by they all faced one another. The boys grinned and waved, looking more at Anna than Harry. One whispered to the other, and they snickered, not unkindly. Harry glanced back at Anna, who blushed furiously. Harry laughed, which only inflamed her embarrassment.

"Sorry Harry, I forgot to tell you about riding on the left hand side if we meet anybody else," she said, in an effort to hide her awkwardness.

"Yeah thanks, you might have mentioned it," he replied.

"I am sorry. I didn't think those boys would come back. I don't know why they did."

"I reckon they came back for a second look," said Harry.

Anna's face reddened again, not that Harry could easily tell, as the suns bathed them in a soft red light anyway. She self-consciously pushed her hair behind her ear, where it remained for all of three seconds.

"When you've quite finished teasing me Harry, you may wish to decide which branch you wish to take ahead of you," she said haughtily.

Harry, although moving slowly on the lower part of the electromagnetic field, had been drifting forwards. He looked ahead and saw the blue line split into two immediately in front of him. There was a slight bump as he arrived at the junction and had little choice but to follow the left hand fork.

"This way I think," he yelled over his shoulder.

"But of course," replied Anna. "I'm sure this is exactly where you wanted to go."

She slid up onto the top of the field and overtook Harry.

"Let's see if you can keep up shall we?" she said as she sped past.

Harry accelerated up onto the top, leaning forward, desperate to keep up. Anna, in spite of her challenge, didn't go too fast, and led on as they wound their way round buildings and through beautifully kept parks. As they went she pointed out places of interest, and soon Harry was able to differentiate between residential, industrial and commercial areas, although the differences were slight. She described how plants grew slower on Tamarisk due to its red and orange suns, so keeping the gardens and parks looking so pretty required little effort once they were established. They traversed several junctions and saw more boarders travelling the invisible highway. Most were swift to move over when they passed by, but there were one or two near misses, usually as a result of younger riders going too fast. Harry was pleased when he and Anna overtook a small group, skimming round them quickly so they didn't lose too much speed. Harry's joy was short lived when he realised it was a group of elderly ladies gliding along slowly but elegantly. He giggled at the sight all the same.

They entered a large park by way of a floral golden archway. A cluster of hillocks, man-made Harry assumed like Terminal Hill, were within the park, and in the centre was one larger hill. It was to this tor they now headed, following the blue lines, weaving their way through the gardens and bumping over the small mounds scattered amongst the trees and ponds, which filled the park.

At the summit they stopped and settled down on a purpose built bench, well placed beneath a soft fronded tree, so they could admire the view and rest their weary forms. Harry's legs ached, and he massaged his calf muscles, as Anna leaned back, swinging her legs and board, while they sat in silence for a couple of minutes. The first sun was halfway to its zenith, and the pursuing second sun was well above the horizon. Their combined red and orange shades gave the surface and buildings of Tamarisk their light reddish tint.

An easy-going wind wound gently round the hilltop, swaying the trees tenderly. There was nobody else in sight.

"We need to talk," said Anna abruptly. "You may not have noticed, but somebody has been following us since we arrived on Tamarisk."

Chapter 10 - Scientists

"Why would anybody want to follow us?" asked Harry. "This doesn't seem that sort of a place. It's so idyllic."

"It does look that way, but we know appearances may often be quite deceiving. Tamarisk is a good place to live, as long as you abide by the rules, which of course most people do."

"You sound like you don't think that's necessarily a good thing," said Harry.

"Don't make me out to be a crook. I'm as much a law abiding citizen as you are!"

"But…"

Anna fell silent again. She looked about them to ensure there was nobody within earshot, but need not have bothered as the nearest people were the two boys they had seen earlier, who were gliding under the park archway.

"Is it them?" asked Harry suspiciously.

"No it's not them. We lost the man who was following when we put on the hover boards. He knew it would be too obvious to come after us that way."

"Does he know you know he's following?"

"Probably," murmured Anna.

"Do we have anything to fear?"

"Not really, but we do need to be careful," Anna said quietly, her mind evidently wandering.

"You're not telling me much," said Harry reproachfully, adding, "In fact, you haven't told me much since we met. I'm all for a bit of mystery, but in my opinion, this tour has gone on long enough."

Anna snapped out of her reverie, and gazed at Harry, who was giving her a serious look.

She laughed. "You are quite right, as always of course. Please accept my apologies. From now on, there'll be no more secrets between us."

"I didn't have any in the first place. I'm just the guy without a family half a galaxy away from home, wondering when he's going to wake up. You're the mystery girl!"

"Really Harry, I am terribly sorry, and I haven't forgotten your recent loss either. I know it can't be easy for you," said Anna. "Remember I've experienced loss as well." She paused. "Which is exactly where we will start."

"Okay," said Harry. "No more secrets though."

"Of course, no more secrets."

Anna took a deep breath and sat back, glancing furtively round them as she did so.

"I think it's time you knew a bit more about what happened to your parents. They didn't always live on Earth you know. Shortly after you were born they lived here on Tamarisk. They came from Earth originally, but were encouraged to emigrate. I don't think anybody ever says 'no' to leaving Earth."

She frowned. "I don't know the details, but I guess they were rescued, in the same way I rescued you."

"From what? I didn't know I needed saving."

"I know, that's the sad part. I rescued you from Earth." She made the word sound dirty.

"What's wrong with Earth? I like it there."

"Oh I know, I'm sorry. I didn't mean it that way, please don't misunderstand me. I love the people of your planet, and it will always be home to you. It's merely there is so much more out here. There's a whole galaxy to explore, and earth-kind haven't got too far yet have they? After all, how many decades has it been since the moon landings, and since then, what?"

Harry felt a little dejected.

"Sorry Harry. I'm no good at this sort of thing. I'm simply excited to think of everything you are going to get to see."

"You said a whole galaxy," said Harry, adding mischievously, "don't you mean the whole Universe?"

"Don't push your luck. Anyway, I was telling you about your parents, if you remember? They were scientists back on Earth, working with atoms and that sort of thing. They came here to work on a project. It was all top secret. You were quite young, so they left you with your grandparents, but I don't think they intended it to be for long. They didn't abandon you or anything like that, and you've seen for yourself how easy it is to come and go between our two worlds. In fact, it's because of them you're automatically entitled to come here.

"Anyway, one day there was a huge explosion at their lab which killed all the scientists instantly. About a dozen people died, but it was all hushed up of course, the same as it would have been on Earth."

"So how do you know all this?" asked Harry.

"My parents also came from Earth, but followed on after yours, working on the next series of experiments some years later. I came with them, but I can't remember much of my life on Earth before we moved, so Tamarisk is my home, even though I wasn't born here.

"At night, I used to listen to my parents talking, which is how I came to learn about your parents. They really were intelligent people, naturally it's from them you inherited your brains."

"What happened to them?" Harry asked quietly. "To your parents, that is."

"They vanished," replied Anna. "I was told they had died in an accident at work, but I was provided with scant details. The Authorities were particularly kind, but said I was too young to understand it all and definitely too young to see their bodies. So to me they just disappeared. That was nearly three years ago."

"How awful," said Harry. "But you've managed to cope. Do you have any other family or friends?"

"A few, and they've been so good to me, but I'm not the easiest person to get on with, and who would want somebody else's teenager living with them. I guess I was a bit of a tearaway. I moved from one family to another for a few months, but made it obvious I would rather be back home. My parents were well paid, so I don't need to work to earn my keep."

"So what do you do with your time?"

"Amongst other things, I like to travel a bit," Anna replied, "and go looking for long lost boys on Earth of course."

"Yes, why did you seek me out?"

Anna looked at him slyly. "Now that question is one I will reserve for when we get home," she whispered.

"Which home would that be?"

"Home number two actually," answered Anna, leaping up and on to the invisible track, where she effortlessly spun round in circles.

Impressed, Harry watched her. "I think I know what you've really been spending your time doing."

"Actually I've always been rather good at this," she answered, as her board stopped spinning, and started up again in the opposite direction, seemingly without any conscious movement from Anna.

"Show off," said Harry, standing up, and slowly easing his board into the magnetic field.

"It's all in the legs," retorted Anna. "Come on, this way," she cried, skimming swiftly away from him.

They circled the top of the tor, slipped over the rim on the far edge and followed a graceful winding route through the scent laden gardens to the bottom, where they dismounted next to some waiting bubble cars. Taking their boards with them, they entered one of the cars, sat down in the comfortable seats, and Anna punched in their destination.

Chapter 11 – The Cellar

That night Harry slept soundly, and awoke to the pleasant sound of a small waterfall in Anna's 'second home'. He lay on his back, hands with fingers locked behind his head, absorbing the delights of a red tinged rainforest, complete with extraordinary little animals scurrying about the jungle floor, colourful fish-filled rock pools, and the cascading waterfall. It was the best awakening he had ever experienced. Harry was wide awake and eager to see what the new day would bring.

"Alarm off," he said, rising from the bed.

Anna had showed him how to set and select the alarm the night before, and how to turn it off. They had arrived at the house in the late afternoon, following another trip in a bubble car, which had taken itself off again, having deposited them on the front doorstep. Anna had been keen to point out that by squinting their eyes, they could see on the horizon the top of the hill in the park where they had been hover-boarding. Harry wasn't convinced, however much he squinted his eyes, but nodded politely all the same.

The house was a single story dwelling, nestled peacefully amongst similar buildings, surrounded as always by well-manicured gardens. Inside it was much larger than the apartment in the cloudscraper, with several reception rooms, and five bedrooms, each with their own bathroom. The house was where Anna had grown up, so held many happy memories, as well as some rather painful ones. Harry was surprised she hadn't moved away to make a fresh start.

Anna provided Harry with a quick tour round the house, showing him how to work the various control panels, and making him feel at home. It was on the whole quite intuitive and he soon learnt what to do, or what to try if he wasn't quite sure. He particularly enjoyed the way the walls lit up and the huge choice of displays, some of which reminded him of exotic places on earth like desert oases, the Grand Canyon and tropical islands. In spite of the range of technological features, it was with dinner Harry was most impressed. They had a take-away, delivered to the door; it was chicken curry. Anna explained that as with the shopping mall it was another thing the Tamariskians had copied from Earth. Exhausted at the end of a long day, there having been twenty hours of daylight from the two suns, Harry had collapsed gratefully into bed.

At Harry's command, the walls turned off, and the sound dropped, but he thought he could still hear the waterfall, before realising it was the sound of a shower in the adjacent room occupied by Anna. Reminded he had his own en-suite facilities he ventured into the bathroom, hoping he could remember how to operate the shower.

A dozen jets of water coming from all directions blasted him, including one from the floor, which Harry had found a little disconcerting, but he decided the shower experience was mostly a pleasurable one. The all over hot air drier was definitely a good thing, and Harry was dressed and ready before Anna had even finished her shower.

Quietly, he headed for the kitchen with the intention of having breakfast ready for when she joined him, but opened the wrong door by mistake, and found himself looking down a flight of steep steps into what must be a cellar. He wondered why Anna hadn't mentioned a basement, and remembered from yesterday's tour he had seen the door, but assumed it was a cupboard. Perhaps his subconscious curiosity had caused him to open the door. Aware the house was now quiet, he realised Anna had finished in the shower, and quickly closed the door, causing it to slam. He winced at the obvious guilty mistake, and fled silently to the kitchen, relieved to hear the noise of Anna's drier starting up.

"Breakfast is served," announced Harry, when Anna finally joined him in the kitchen. Laid out on the table was a typical Tamarisk style breakfast; two plates with several nondescript looking dried shapes of varying colours and two glasses of clear liquid. Harry had found a bottle in the fridge, the colourless contents of which had smelt slightly orangey, and he hoped were fit for human consumption.

"Well, Harry," exclaimed Anna, "you really have outdone yourself. We'll make a Tamariskian of you yet."

"I found a packet, which said Breakfast, so took a huge gamble and decided to serve it first."

Laughing, they sat down to eat. Harry watched to make sure Anna drank from her glass first, and seeing there were no adverse side-effects, assumed it was safe to drink. He took a sip and found it to be like the orange juice he was familiar with at home.

"So," he said, "when are we going to have a look in the cellar?" He had decided not to even attempt to hide his earlier discovery.

"Oh, you found the old lab did you?"

"No, I opened the wrong door, trying to find my way to the kitchen, and happened to see the steps leading down. Did your parents used to have a laboratory under the house?"

Anna nodded. "Not used to, it's still there," she said.

With breakfast finished they descended into the cellar down the steep steps, which opened out into a large well lit room. There were several benches dotted about, with impressive looking apparatus in various states of build.

"Take a look round," said Anna, gesturing about the room.

Harry walked up to the first bench, and looked more closely at the bits and pieces scattered around. A few things looked similar to the fixings used on Earth, and these he found grouped in small pots, but the remaining items were quite alien to him. He could see some parts rotated, but couldn't locate any source of power.

Anna watched him silently, chewing slightly on her lower lip and tucking her errant hair behind her ear.

"Look at this over here," she said, moving over to the third bench. "My dad made it for me years ago."

Harry looked and saw built onto the top of the bench a track similar to the slot car racing track he had in his bedroom at home. Two miniature hoverboards lay beside the track. He watched as Anna pushed a button on a black box, picked up the boards and tossed them onto the track, where an electromagnetic field immediately captured them. The boards sat, levitating a little above the track, emitting a slight humming sound. Harry cried out with delight, feeling quite young all of a sudden at the prospect of playing with a new toy.

"Put your index fingers on the two marks on the bench in front of you," instructed Anna.

Harry looked down, and seeing two small star-like red symbols, he did as instructed.

"Move your left finger to control your speed, and your right to execute tricks."

He slid his left finger forward, and the board nearest to him whirred more loudly, and skipped off joyfully around the track, floating as serenely as had Harry on the real thing. The little board banked around the corners and bobbed up and down over the humps. Moving his right finger around, Harry experimented with the controls and found he could make his board spin and by tapping lightly, it performed a series of little jumps.

Anna's own board started to move, and Harry noted it was not doing any tricks, but was accelerating rapidly. He grinned and turned up the speed of his own board, keeping his eyes on the track, his competitive side not wanting to make any mistakes and lose too easily. Anna's board had been gaining on his own quite quickly, but now he had his up to full speed she was struggling to catch up. They raced round and round the track, a complete circuit only taking a few seconds, the boards almost a blur.

Anna laughed. "You're only winning because you have the inside line Harry."

He noted she was telling the truth, so refrained from protesting.

"At least, you have for now," she added, and did a quick double tap with her left hand as her board hit the top of bump before a bend. It jumped neatly across onto the invisible rail that guided Harry's own board.

"No, you can't do that," yelped Harry.

Anna's board had nearly caught up, but as both boards rounded the steepest bend, they leapt off the track, sailed past Anna's head and across the room, until they crashed into the far wall.

"Lethal!" cried Harry.

"They always come off that bend eventually," explained Anna.

"Funnily enough, so do my cars back on Earth," said Harry.

Anna switched off the power to the race track, while Harry retrieved the wayward boards. Picking them up off the floor on the opposite side of the room, he turned to see Anna in the far corner on all fours, and reaching into a rather dirty looking cupboard. She pulled out an old tool box, which might well have come from Earth, stretched her hands further in, going so far only her legs protruded from the cupboard. Harry placed the boards next to the track and went to see what Anna was up to.

"Are you sure you're quite alright down there?" he asked, laughing at the comical sight.

His mocking was short-lived, as he watched Anna's whole body disappear. He knelt down and peered into the murk, unable to make any sense of what was happening. "Lights on." Anna's voice sounded from the darkness, and a bright light lit up the cupboard, which he could see opened out into another room.

"Nice one, a secret passageway," Harry said to himself, dropping to his knees and crawling into the cupboard.

Chapter 12 – The Secret Lab

The passageway opened out into a second musty smelling cellar, which was roughly the same size as the first. It was another lab, but unlike the other, the workbenches lined the walls, and drawn in the middle of the floor was a ring, in which three small devices mounted on tripods pointed gun-like towards the centre of the circle.

Anna was turning on a side wall, which displayed an assortment of camera views of the outside of the house, and the approach.

"So, what do you think?" Anna asked, spreading her arms out grandly.

"I think it's most impressive," declared Harry. "What is it?"

"It, as you so delicately put it, is a science laboratory."

"I can see that," said Harry, warming to the conversation, "but what is it?"

"Yeah, alright. Come over here and I shall explain." She pointed to a mark on the floor which was directly in the line of sight of the three devices.

"If sir would care to step onto this spot here," she said gracefully.

"No, sir would not care to, actually," said Harry bluntly, eying the arrangement doubtfully. "How do I know you won't shoot me or something?"

Anna sighed, "You're not particularly trusting are you?" adding, "which I suppose isn't necessarily too bad a thing."

She showed Harry to a series of box mounted controls on one of the benches. A wall-screen displayed an array of outputs from the controls; graphs, wavy lines, and flashing messages Harry could not understand. Cables dropped away from the equipment and slithered across the floor to connect with the tripods and their suspicious looking contraptions.

"This is the lab where my parents worked, when they weren't at work," explained Anna. "It's all completely illegal of course. All scientific research on Tamarisk is controlled by the Authorities, and anybody caught conducting their own experiments at home is prosecuted and permanently banned from all research jobs.

"My parents' specialist field was in wormhole technology, like the space portal. They were investigating alternative uses, and different ways of creating wormholes. At present, the space portals require huge amounts of power to keep them open, and the portals themselves are not exactly small."

Harry interrupted, "Actually, I've been meaning to ask you. Where does your energy come from?"

"It's all solar power here. All of the buildings use photovoltaic materials in their construction, which convert the sunlight into electricity. This in turn is stored in batteries hidden in the walls, and run many of our appliances by induction. I expect you've studied this in your physics lessons."

"A little," Harry ventured.

"It doesn't matter. We take energy for granted nowadays."

"So why were your parents conducting illegal experiments at home in their cellar?" Harry asked, returning to the original subject.

"As you know, they weren't exactly open with me. I knew all about the secret lab, and I wasn't to mention a word about it to anyone. But I believe they stumbled upon your own parents' research at work, and when they tried to explore it further the Authorities forced them to stop. So of course, they carried on at home instead."

Anna was about to continue, when one of the walls flashed alarmingly, displaying a view of the outside of the house. A bubble car had pulled up, and a lone figure stepped from the vehicle.

"Oh no, we have an unwelcome visitor," groaned a troubled looking Anna.

Chapter 13 – The Unwelcome Visit

Anna jumped into action, switching off the images on the wall. "Quick, back into the main lab, turn on the hover board track and start playing," she instructed. "I'll bring him down in a minute. He's bound to want to see you."

"But who is he?" asked Harry, scrambling through the secret passage.

"He's from the Authorities, he's the man who was following us yesterday. He'll pretend to be friendly, so just respond in kind, but he is absolutely not to be trusted," she replied. "He's tricky, this one! Lights off."

A pleasant bird-like noise chirruped throughout the house, which Harry took to be the doorbell. Anna followed Harry out of the dark cupboard and threw the old toolbox into it, swung the door shut, replaced the bench and rushed to the steps that led back up to the ground floor.

Harry powered up the hover board race track. He took up position at the controls which placed him with his back to the stairs. He set the board off slowly, straining his ears over the quiet hum of the hovering toy. He heard the door open and Anna's voice sounded out clearly, but he struggled to hear what the man was saying.

"Oh hi, this is a nice surprise," Anna said enthusiastically. "Come on in. No, I was in the cellar. That's alright. Why don't you come down?"

Harry swore under his breath, feeling stressed. He accelerated the board, so it made more noise and he could pretend he was unaware anyone was descending the steps. He heard them reach the bottom, one after the other.

"Err, Harry," said Anna, coughing politely behind him. "We have a guest."

He removed his hands from the touch controls and turned round to face the man from the Authorities.

"Sorry," said Harry appearing embarrassed. "I didn't hear you come down." He had decided quiet and shy was probably the best way to appear. It wouldn't be difficult, and would hopefully mask his nervousness.

The man from the Authorities was not at all as Harry had expected. He was of average build and height, wore casual clothes and a pleasant expression, he had a friendly air about him, and smiled warmly at Harry.

"Harry, this is Rience," explained Anna. "He's an old friend. Rience has looked out for me ever since I lost my parents." She rested her head briefly on the man's shoulder. Rience patted Anna affectionately on her arm, but to Harry their show of friendliness towards one another didn't quite ring true.

"It's a pleasure to meet you young man," said Rience, offering his hand for Harry to shake. Harry returned the greeting.

"So you're from Earth, Harry," he said matter-of-factly.

Harry wondered if he had given himself away with the hand shake; he was unsure how people greeted one another on Tamarisk, before remembering that at the Arrivals Hall he had seen some people grasping one another's wrists rather than their hands. He could have kicked himself, but decided it was probably better he didn't pretend to be anyone other than himself, and to keep quiet instead. He remembered somebody famous once saying it was better to say nothing at all than to open one's mouth and give oneself away, or was it something to do with appearing foolish? Harry couldn't quite remember but whatever it was, it sounded like good advice.

Rience continued, "So what do you think of Tamarisk?"

"Impressive," replied Harry. "It seems quiet, I like that."

"Oh good, so do I. I've been to Earth several times, although perhaps not quite as many as our mutual friend here," said Rience, jerking his head towards Anna, who had been fixing Harry with a serious look. She quickly smiled back. "But I always enjoy returning to the peace and quiet of Tamarisk," he added. "We prefer a more gentle way of life here, don't you think Anna?" He kept his eyes fixed on Harry.

"Oh definitely," agreed Anna. "Earth is an exciting place to visit, but it's always nice to come home again."

Harry decided to chip in, "I've had enough excitement recently. A bit of calm and relaxation is what I need."

"Indeed, Harry," Rience nodded appreciatively. "Be careful though that Anna doesn't get you into anything silly like hoverboarding, that's all."

Harry felt uneasy; he was fairly sure Rience must already know where they had been and what they had been doing.

"Oh I've tried it already. That's why I need a rest," explained Harry, adding, "I don't think my calf muscles will ever recover." He rubbed his right leg melodramatically. This lying business is getting pretty easy, he thought, as long as I don't overdo it. He smiled at Rience and Anna, attempting to appear as natural as possible.

Rience met his gaze. "Alright, okay," he said good naturedly, beaming at the pair. "You've had your bit of fun, but I'm afraid now we are going to have to get a bit serious."

He fixed them both with a solemn look, and Harry turned to Anna, a puzzled expression on his face. Anna shrugged her shoulders.

"Now come on young lady, don't be like that," cajoled Rience. "You know very well you haven't been following the rules."

Anna adopted an air of innocence, shifting her weight casually onto one leg, and blowing up at her hair from the corner of her mouth. She wrinkled her brow in thought. "I can't really remember doing anything wrong."

"Oh Anna, but you didn't seek permission to bring Harry here, did you. And you haven't registered him with the Authorities either, have you?"

"I know but I was going to register him first thing tomorrow. I didn't think he would want to go through all that on his first day. Of course, now you're here, you can do it for us, can't you?" she suggested amiably.

"Yes, I suppose so," replied Rience, "but you know you should have sought authorisation first."

"I know, I'm sorry," said Anna guiltily. "But there wasn't enough time. They were going to send him away to a children's home, and his grandfather had only just died. It didn't seem right to me, and so I wanted to do the best for Harry. And haven't you always told me to think more about others rather than myself?"

Rience smiled sweetly, a little too sickly Harry thought, and he felt uneasy. "Of course dear girl, you are quite right, but you must remember rules are rules, and you are not above them."

Rience took Harry's details, such as his Earth address, and date of arrival on Tamarisk, and entered them onto a portable device he produced from an inside pocket of his jacket. Harry felt quite tense as Rience asked his questions, but it was Anna who answered, and she gave honest replies to them all.

The formality of registering Harry over, they went upstairs and bade Rience goodbye from the doorway.

"Don't go far," he cautioned them. "I may need to ask a few more questions. You know what the Authorities are like for demanding accuracy, so I hope you haven't made any mistakes. Oh, and I'll send Sorrel round tomorrow with your visa Harry, giving you permission to stay for six months."

Rience gave them a cheerful wave, as he climbed into a waiting bubble car. They returned his wave and closed the door.

Chapter 14 – Bugged

Harry breathed a huge sigh of relief, and slumped back against the wall. Anna also let out a sigh, but put one finger over her lips and beckoned to him to follow her back down into the cellar. Once there she crouched down and looked under the mini hove board table. Anna frowned and Harry followed the line of her finger to where he could see a small black disc stuck to the underneath of the bench. He opened his mouth in surprise, but refrained from gasping; it could only be a listening bug of some kind.

On returning quietly to the kitchen, Anna pressed a button on the wall, and instantaneously hot water spluttered boisterously from a small tap into a jug placed beneath it.

"The range on that thing is good enough to hear us anywhere in the house," she whispered under the cover of the noisy water. "Behave naturally for a couple of hours, after which we'll go and sort out that sneaky device."

Harry nodded and mouthed, "Okay." He could feel his heart beating rapidly; he knew Rience couldn't be trusted, but now he wondered what he had got himself into.

The jug filled, the water turned off automatically, and Anna added the powdery contents of a small packet, which rapidly dissolved.

"I'm sure you'll like this," she said, in what Harry regarded as the most ordinary sounding voice he had ever heard. It seemed to him

Anna was unnaturally relaxed with the situation, and clearly she was quite used to this kind of subterfuge.

All he could manage was a rather pathetic sounding, "Sure."

Anna poured the drink into two mugs, both of which were from Earth Harry noticed. One had the words 'I went to London and all I got was this lousy mug' on the side, and the other had a picture of the Leaning Tower of Pisa, which would ironically appear upright when the user tipped it to drink.

"Come on, let's go and relax," said Anna warmly, carrying the mugs through to the living room.

They spent the next couple of hours chatting amiably, comparing the merits of Earth and Tamarisk, and flicking through the channels grandiosely displayed on one of the walls. Harry found it exhausting, having become overtly self-conscious, due to the knowledge that Rience, and who knew who else, were most likely listening in on their every word.

Finally, Anna stood up and proposed they return to the cellar for a hoverboard re-match, to give Harry the chance to beat her. Back in the cellar, Anna took a large magnet from a draw, and suggested to Harry he might like to turn on the track. As he did so, she placed the magnet up against the listening device, which gave out a pitiful little pop.

"Right, that's fixed that," declared Anna triumphantly, and for the second time that day Harry let out a huge sigh of relief.

"So, does Rience think we're up to no good?"

"Of course he does."

"Why should he suspect anything at all?"

"For two reasons really. One, because he's good at his job, and so is Sorrel, we must be on our toes when he drops in tomorrow. And secondly, because he's right, we are up to something, or at least, we will be."

"And what exactly are we going to be getting up to?" asked Harry suspiciously.

"Simple. We are going to get to the bottom of what happened to my parents," replied Anna, adding, "and also to your own."

"Oh," said Harry flatly, "okay."

Chapter 15 – Alive

The two friends returned to the main part of the house. Anna was concerned somebody may be watching them from outside, so they continued to behave normally, by flicking through some of the channels on the wall-screen. They watched the news for a short while, but were soon bored. Channel hopping again, they stumbled across an interesting history program, not normally one of Harry's favourite subjects, but it gave him a brief insight into Tamarisk's past. There hadn't been a war for over four hundred years, ever since having a 'war to end all wars'.

Unlike Earth's similarly named First World War, the name was appropriate, due to the nuclear weapons used causing so many deaths, and the subsequent peace treaties preventing any possible repetition of the conflict. It took two hundred years for the planet to recover to a point where people no longer died from radiation sickness, and for industrial growth to start over again. Finally galvanised into action, Tamarisk had prospered, with lessons learned from the many mistakes made before the war.

The programme continued; seventy five years ago, a scientist attempting to develop a new source of electrical power inadvertently opened a small worm hole. Unfortunately for him, he promptly fell in and nobody had seen the unlucky chap since. Fortunately though for the rest of Tamarisk, his colleagues who witnessed the event had been taking notes, and in time were able to recreate the wormhole. Some thirty years later stable wormholes, which could support the passage of people to destinations of reasonable choice became the norm, and speedy interplanetary travel was born.

The first Tamariskian wormhole travellers quickly made friends with peaceful humanoids on other planets who, keen to make use of the new travel network readily traded their technology, such as the invisibility cloak used round the ring of stones on Earth, solar power and even the hoverboards, which came from a planet almost entirely dedicated to providing amusements to the rest of the known galaxy. Harry thought it sounded not unlike a planet-size version of Blackpool, where he had once been with his grandparents when he was young; it had rained. Unsurprisingly, due to the myriad of delights on offer, it rapidly became a favourite destination for the inhabitants of many worlds, (the Pleasure Planet that is, not Blackpool), and also the home to the wealthiest of people. Harry glanced expectantly at Anna lounging beside him as they watched, enthralled by the vast array of entertainment available.

"One day Harry," she said without looking at him, "one day. You'll love the speedboards."

The wormholes had literally opened doors to virtually unlimited if rather random possibilities for exploration. Not all had been successful, and there were a number of deaths early on, particularly when advance parties encountered hostile locals all too keen to take the wormhole technology for themselves. Instead, they had the door slammed permanently shut in their faces, leaving them with the frustration of knowing their greed had lost them so much.

After several years the wormholes brought the explorers to Earth. The screen displayed archive footage of the first discreet human contact and the subsequent return visit to Tamarisk. Harry smiled, as it reminded him of the early jerky black and white films of explorers meeting remote Amazonian tribes, only this time it was the developed peoples of Earth that appeared uncivilised.

Somewhat disturbingly for Harry, the narrator went on to explain why travel via space portal was unavailable to most Earthlings, due to their warring nature, and so to date mostly only scientists of a passive disposition had made the trip.

Anna sensed his unease, but merely shrugged her shoulders. "You can't argue with that," she said bluntly.

Begrudgingly, Harry was compelled to agree, but felt quite defensive of his home, pointing out that if the rulers there knew what the reward for world peace would be, they would stop all conflicts overnight.

"True," admitted Anna, "but shouldn't peace in itself be the reward for ending all fighting."

Harry felt quite dejected, knowing what she said was true. He no longer felt quite so proud of his little planet.

The programme ended with a whistle-stop tour of the galaxy encompassing all of the planets currently available to visit, and with the end credits were displayed potential other worlds yet to be discovered.

Anna was quiet for a while, before saying softly, "I don't believe my parents died in an accident."

"Neither do I," said Harry, "they were murdered, weren't they? Because they were getting too close to finding out about what happened to my parents."

"Actually no," she replied, which surprised Harry. "I think my parents are still alive, but transported somewhere else, or are maybe trapped in some kind of state of limbo."

"I'm sorry Anna, but isn't that simply wishful thinking?" Harry said gently.

Anna sighed and looked at Harry. "I didn't think like this in the beginning. I accepted they were dead, but always assumed, as you had, that somebody had killed them. And yet the further I looked into their research, and the more I thought about their sudden disappearance, the more likely it seemed to me they really had vanished into thin air.

"The problem was the Authorities claimed my parents died at their workplace, but I'm sure they said they were going to work from home that day. I was out hoverboarding, no great surprise I know, and when I returned home the place was empty. And I already told you the Authorities cleared out all my parents stuff in the cellar. They did all that before I arrived home. But the secret lab remained exactly that, a secret. All I know is it definitely doesn't add up.

"I know what you're thinking. That I'm giving myself false hope, but I'm not. The thought that they might be trapped somewhere, unable to do anything, but perhaps remaining conscious these last three years, is more unbearable than when I thought they were dead. If anything, I almost wish I hadn't considered the possibility at all."

Harry agreed, the idea was not at all pleasant.

"I once spent an hour in detention, and that was bad enough," he said, slumping down in his seat.

Anna laughed loudly. "Oh, thank you Harry, I was beginning to feel quite morose."

Harry raised his eyebrows. "Morose, is it?" he asked.

Anna grinned. "It's my big word for today."

They fell silent and Harry yawned. The thirty hour Tamarisk day was beginning to feel quite long, particularly with the range of emotions he had experienced. He felt his eyes begin to close.

"Harry, there is one other thing I have to tell you."

Harry snapped his head back up, and opened his eyes.

"I once heard my dad say your parents were the only ones not found after the explosion. I think your mum and dad are alive as well, caught up in the same place as my own parents. It's why I sought you out Harry and it's the real reason I need you here. You're going to help me and together we're going to bring back our parents."

Chapter 16 – Conundrum

They had an early supper, over which Anna described how, the day after her parent's supposed death, people had come and removed the rest of the research they had at home. What they didn't know was Anna's parents had taken copies of all their notes, and safely hidden it away in the secret lab, complete with several prototypes of the equipment on which they had been working.

"I need your help with a complex conundrum I can't seem to crack," explained Anna. "It's a little bit of mathematics, similar to the calculus you learn on Earth. But I believe if we can understand what our parents were on to we'll be able to get the wormhole equipment working and solve the mystery of their disappearance."

"What's calculus?" queried Harry.

"Oh of course, you haven't got that far yet, but you have done algebra?"

Harry nodded.

"Of course you have, everybody does algebra, even if they don't realise it. Well it's like that - only more so."

"Right," said Harry hesitantly. "But can't we get help from anyone else?"

"No definitely not, it's far too risky. We can't trust anyone. This technology would be far too dangerous in the wrong hands, but worse still, there are those who would stop at nothing to prevent it from happening at all."

"I don't understand why."

"It's like oil on your world. You have the ability to live without it, the same as we do here, but Earth's economy would collapse without it. The changeover needs to be gradual of course, but there are too many people making it far too gradual, because they would lose their powerful positions if Earth instantly had free re-usable energy."

Harry felt quite overawed and a little sceptical about the importance Anna was placing on their task, and he thought her somewhat paranoid with all the cloak and dagger antics, but decided not to mention it.

"Come on, I'll show you, after which we can get started."

She led the way back down to the cellar and through the hidden passage to the secret laboratory. From one of the cupboards she removed several stacks of paper, all covered in outlandish symbols, which quickly changed in front of Harry's eyes as the universal translator did its job.

"I've been reading this lot for the last two years, and have made plenty of progress. I'm sure I'm close to understanding it, but I've got a bit stuck and can't quite get my head round some parts. I suspect you're far cleverer than me, so now it's over to you Harry."

"I don't think so," said Harry, thumbing through some of the papers. "I don't understand any of this."

"Not at the moment you don't, but in time I'm sure you will," Anna encouraged him. "Your parents were geniuses! They solved the problem."

"But I don't even know what the problem is," sighed Harry.

"Oh yes sorry, I forgot to say. It's the science behind how wormholes work," stated Anna.

"But you people have been using wormholes here for decades. How can you not know how they work?" asked Harry incredulously.

"Remember, they were discovered by accident," Anna explained patiently. "With a little science they were stabilised, but even now nobody really knows the proper physics behind them. At least nobody knew until your parents figured it out, and mine as well apparently."

"Wow, that's amazing," said Harry.

"I know, pretty cool huh, but there's more." Anna cast her hand over the piles of research. "From what I can tell, there's some sort of fifth dimension, a kind of mixture of time and space, and that's where wormholes come in."

"It all seems a bit vague."

"Don't I know it, but that's why you're here." Anna smiled encouragingly at Harry, who sighed dejectedly.

"Well I don't know Anna. You're placing a great deal of trust in my ability to achieve things in subjects I know nothing about."

"I have faith, that's all. You only need to have some confidence. There's no pressure, think of this as puzzle solving."

"No pressure you say," said Harry smirking. "All you want is for me to help you bring our parents back to life."

"Exactly, dead easy huh?"

"You're not funny."

That first night they worked late, occasionally taking a break for a drink or snack, until finally giving in to sleep and going to bed long after both suns had set.

They awoke refreshed the next morning, and following a quick breakfast returned enthusiastically to their work. Anna produced some more equipment from another cupboard and another bundle of papers.

"I like the way, with all this futuristic technology, your parents liked to tie their research together with string."

Anna agreed. "I think it must be a scientist joke or something, an appreciation for the irony of using such an arcane method to store their modern records."

Eagerly, Anna showed Harry the new equipment, which was something else her parents had been working on. She explained how, in theory, it would create a field around the user, which acted a bit like a shield.

"A field shield, I like the sound of that," chuckled Harry.

Anna laughed. "Seriously though, if this works it could be more dangerous than any weapon."

"How?"

"Because the greatest type of weapon is a shield," stated Anna.

"I think you've lost the plot completely now."

"No I haven't, think about it for a minute. If you have a shield that can defend against a weapon, you can always retaliate later."

"I suppose so," Harry agreed reluctantly.

"This shield however can defend against any weapon," Anna continued. "It can distort space and time, swallowing literally anything, like a miniature wormhole."

"So it doesn't reflect, it absorbs, but where do the bullets and other things go when they enter the wormhole?"

"Anywhere you want them to, like into the heart of the nearest sun, or out into deep space."

"Or even straight back at the person who attacked you," added Harry quietly.

"Now you're getting it," Anna said seriously.

Harry went on. "Bullets, explosives, energy. Anything could be absorbed. Armed with only a small weapon, the wearer of one of these field shields could do untold damage. He would quite literally be a one man army! But that's amazing. How does it work?"

"That's the dilemma, it doesn't," said Anna dejectedly, "or at least, I can't get it to work, although I don't think my parents could either. They were concentrating mostly on the portal technology. There's this one particular area I can't get my head round. I don't understand what it is or does or anything. I can't see how it has anything to do with the rest of the calculations, it's just tagged on. I'm hoping you'll have more luck."

They returned to their work, sifting through the new pile of research, sometimes leaping on excitedly, and often lapsing into silence, either reading the next page or lost in their own thoughts. Eventually they stopped for lunch and a rest, after which Harry dozed briefly, acutely aware of the longer days on Tamarisk.

"You know, wormholes aren't an exact science. So far most have been opened at the intersection of planetary energy lines," said Anna, back in the lab.

"You don't mean ley lines, do you?" cried Harry. "They're a load of old rubbish."

"Usually I would be inclined to agree, but you have to wonder if there's something in it. The portal at the centre of the Ring of Stones on Earth surely isn't merely a coincidence," Anna pointed out.

Harry mused for a moment. "Perhaps they're weak lines of magnetism."

"Some believe pigeons can detect magnetic fields, and use them to navigate."

"Personally I think they follow the roads."

"And follow the road signs of course, they're clever birds."

"Did you ever report your ideas?" asked Harry earnestly, changing the subject and the mood.

"I was only joking about the pigeons," Anna answered slyly.

Harry fixed her with a blank stare, his eyebrows only slightly raised.

"Oh you probably mean my ideas about what happened to my parents, don't you?" Anna said mischievously. "Not the pigeons."

Harry refused to take the bait, and instead raised his eyebrows a little further.

"Well yes, of course you do. How absolutely silly of me," she said.

Harry couldn't help but be amused by Anna's playfulness.

"I went to the Authorities, but they wouldn't listen," she finally answered Harry's question.

"There was one woman who was a friend of my parents. Her name's Emma, I stayed with her for a little while. She was sympathetic and listened to everything I told her, but I could tell she didn't believe a word I said. She advised me not to mention it to anyone until I had hard evidence. I think it was her way of avoiding the subject. It's quite reasonable, I don't blame her at all. Everyone was terribly upset at the time."

They returned once more to the task at hand, Anna showing Harry yet another bundle of papers, this time covered with unusual markings, of which Harry could make no sense whatsoever.

"I don't understand this," he moaned.

"Come on, let me show you. Look at these symbols here."

"I don't think the universal translator is working. They don't mean anything to me. What's this character here?" asked Harry, pointing to a peculiar curly looking symbol.

"I think it's some sort of adjustment, or an offset of sorts, but for what, I'm really not sure. That's been my biggest headache from the start. I don't think they can be translated, because it's all stuff which hasn't been discovered on Earth yet, but I'm sure you'll get the hang of it. Look at this first line here, both sides have to balance, so whatever you apply to one part, you need to do to the other side as well."

"Like algebraic equations."

"Very similar. Now look at this second line."

Chapter 17 – Sorrel

The following morning Harry slept in quite late; unaccustomed to the long Tamariskian days he slept more soundly, but awoke all the more refreshed for a good night's sleep. He showered, helped himself to breakfast, and joined Anna in the lab.

Half way through the morning, they stopped for a snack, which they ate in the kitchen. As they were finishing, there was a knock at the door.

Anna swore under her breath. "It must be Sorrel with your visa, and we've left the lab open. Oh well, there isn't time to do anything now. We'll just have to wing it, and hope he doesn't want to go downstairs."

Anna led the way, quietly closing the cellar door as they passed. A short man with a silly grin greeted them warmly as they opened the front door.

"Anna," the beaming man cried out with delight. Sorrel stepped through the doorway and hugged her fiercely.

"Hello Sorrel, it's good to see you again," Anna said through clenched teeth as she strained against the overtly friendly greeting.

"And this of course is your friend Harry." Sorrel pumped Harry's hand furiously, beaming all the while. "All the way from Earth, how wonderful. You must take me there one day Anna. I've heard so many wonderful things about the place." He chortled loudly. "Surfing, that's what I want to have a go at."

Anna and Harry couldn't help but laugh along with him, his infectious manner effortlessly lifting their spirits. Anna closed the door and Sorrel took a deep breath and looked around him excitedly. He gestured towards the cellar door.

"I guess I'll have to settle for a spot of table hoverboarding for now. Fancy another thrashing young lady, or what about you young man?" he said turning to Harry encouragingly.

Harry felt the colour drain from his face. "Er, I'm not sure, it's up to Anna," he spluttered.

"Sorry Sorrel, maybe another time" said Anna putting her arm around his shoulders and guiding him towards the living room. "I'm afraid it stopped working yesterday. I think something may be interfering with the controls, but I haven't had a chance to fix it yet."

Harry sighed inwardly, how does she do it so easily, he wondered?

"Of course we could always go out a bit later, and have a go at the real thing," suggested Anna, tucking her wayward hair behind her ear, as they settled down on the comfortable chairs.

Sorrel chuckled, "You'll get me into trouble, you will Anna."

"Well it wouldn't be the first time would it? Rience doesn't approve of such things," Anna explained to Harry.

"Ah, speaking of whom." Sorrel reached into an inside pocket of his jacket and produced a small plastic card, and handed it to Harry. "Your visa sir, as requested," he declared with a flourish.

Harry took it and studied the holographic picture of his head which appeared to hover above the card, and move about as he twisted it.

"Pretty cool, thanks Sorrel." He accepted the card graciously.

There followed a rather uncomfortable silence, as Sorrel clearly had no intention of leaving yet, making himself quite at home, and looking about himself as though he was missing something.

"Er, may I offer you a drink?" asked Anna, guessing at Sorrel's need.

"Thank you my dear, yes please, a hot coffee would do nicely," he replied graciously.

"I'll make it," snapped Harry, jumping to his feet, desperate not to be alone with the man from the Authorities.

"Oh thanks Harry," said Anna. "You know where everything is, give me a shout if you need any help." She turned to Sorrel. "Coffee is always served hot, so you don't need to ask for it that way," she explained.

"Ah well you know best Anna," said Sorrel, raising both hands out to her, before clasping them together meekly. "I bow to your superior Earth knowledge. It was a poor attempt by me to appear clever. I must go there one day, and savour some of the delights the place has to offer."

Anna gave him a shrewd look. "In which case there may be something you can help me with. Harry and I may need to return to Earth in the next few days, only briefly of course, but you are welcome to join us."

"Thanks Anna, that would be nice, what a wonderful idea," said Sorrel joyously. "Of course, I'll have to check with Rience first."

"Well I'm sure he won't mind. Now Harry will need a cloaking add on for his translator."

"We're not meant to give them out to first time visitors."

"So how is Harry to get back? He can't exactly walk out of thin air when he leaves George's hub now, can he?"

"True I guess," said Sorrel hesitantly, scratching his chin. "Why do you need to return to Earth anyway?"

"Ah well, that's something else I wanted to ask you about," said Anna seriously. "Do you have your inter-world browser on you?"

In the kitchen, Harry finished making the coffee, which he brought through on a tray, with a small pot of milk. He had explored the cupboards and found a bewildering array of foodstuffs, including quite a few from Earth, including coffee, sugar and the milk, which was in a fridge of sorts. When he put in his hand, it had not felt cold, but the contents of the fridge certainly did.

"Neat fridge," Harry said to Anna, grinning as he entered. Both she and Sorrel abruptly stopped talking and looked up at him.

"I thought you'd like it, and before you ask, no I don't know how it works."

"Milk and sugar?" Harry asked Sorrel, placing the tray on a low table in front of the jolly little man, who peered inquisitively at the offerings.

"Only one cup! Are you two not having anything?" Sorrel poured in three drops of milk followed by three spoonfuls of sugar, but didn't stir it in.

"No, we only finished lunch shortly before you arrived," answered Harry, feeling more at ease around the man from the Authorities, who didn't appear at all austere like Rience. In truth he had made only one coffee because he didn't want to give Sorrel any excuse to stay longer than necessary. "And besides," he continued, "we're keen to get straight back to work."

He could have kicked himself.

"Really," exclaimed Sorrel. "Whatever are you two working on?" he enquired, sitting forward in his chair, sipping intently at his coffee, and peering at them over the rim of the cup.

Anna stepped in as always. "We're attempting to get the hoverboard table back up and running, of course. Didn't I tell you earlier? Really Sorrel, you must learn to pay attention or you'll never get anywhere at the Authorities," she said cheekily.

Harry nodded enthusiastically, eternally grateful Anna's quick thinking had saved him yet again.

Sorrel fixed Anna with a look that spoke volumes, while she in turn sat with an air of sublime innocence.

"If you were my daughter..." he started.

"Then you can be grateful I'm not," Anna finished for him.

He chuckled and took another sip of his coffee. "I think that was my cue to leave," he said, gulping down the rest of his drink.

From the sharp look of distaste on Sorrel's face, Harry assumed he must have reached the undissolved sugar sitting in the bottom of the cup.

"Nice coffee Harry, thank you," Sorrel said through slightly pursed lips.

"My pleasure," replied Harry, unable to hide a knowing smile.

They showed Sorrel to the front door, where he energetically shook Harry's hand once again, and attempted to squeeze the life out of Anna, who whimpered painfully. Harry noted Sorrel darted a quick look at the cellar door.

"Don't worry, we'll get the hoverboard table up and working again," said Harry sharply.

"I'm sure you will," chuckled Sorrel, "I'm sure you will."

They closed the door behind him, and this time it was Anna who let out a sigh of relief.

"Can we talk?" Harry mouthed silently.

"Yes, I didn't take my eyes off him, so even had he wanted to bug us, I didn't give him the opportunity. By the way, well done on spotting him looking at the cellar door."

"Thanks, I messed up earlier though," mumbled Harry sheepishly, "and you had to come to my rescue again."

"Don't worry about it. The Authorities don't have a clue what we're doing."

"Does Sorrel know we know?"

"Does he know we know what?"

"That we know he knows something, even if he doesn't know what it is."

"Oh probably," Anna responded calmly, "but I doubt he knows we know that as well. Clear…?"

"…As mud!" Harry completed. "He seemed genuinely friendly though."

"All the more reason not to trust him, don't you think?"

"I suppose so. But you two seem to get on quite well."

"It's quite patronising of him really. Him and Rience both," said Anna tartly. "They like to portray themselves as protective uncles, like the Authorities are one big happy family. Did you hear his rubbish about hot coffee? He must think I'm stupid to think for one minute I would actually believe him when he says he doesn't know how to make coffee. He may be telling the truth about not having visited Earth, but I know for a fact everyone at the Authorities drinks coffee. They have it brought over from Earth especially. I remember my parents talking about it."

"But what about the sugar?"

"Merely a simple ruse to make us think he's some kind of bumbling idiot, when he's anything but. We need to be careful."

"Perhaps tomorrow we should go out and do normal stuff," suggested Harry. Anna nodded and Harry changed the subject. "So what were you two talking about when I came back into the room?"

"I asked Sorrel to check on something on Earth for me. He has a device which can access Earth's internet," Anna explained. "Harry, it's your grandfather's funeral in a few days' time. I think you ought to attend."

"I know, I've been thinking about that myself," said Harry softly. "I don't think I'd ever forgive myself if I didn't go."

Chapter 18 – Wind Up

The next day they took a break from their covert activities in the secret laboratory to go hoverboarding again. There was a stiff breeze in the air as they exited Anna's house with their boards tucked under their arms, and climbed into the bubble car they had requested several minutes earlier.

"This wind gives me an idea," said Anna mysteriously, but despite Harry's instance, she refused to let on.

"It's unkind to lead people on that way," Harry scolded her.

"I expect you're right, but I want you to enjoy the surprise," she countered, and punched in a new destination on the bubble car's controls.

Harry reclined in the big seat and watched the world flash past. It was a beautiful place, the way town and country seemed to blend together as one, although he found the lack of proper open countryside a little claustrophobic.

The trip lasted only a few minutes, ending with their arrival at a large open red-tinted grassy area, which contrasted significantly with the rest of the land. Given Harry's thoughts a few moments earlier he considered it quite a coincidence. As they stepped out of the bubble car, in the distance he could vaguely make out small sail-like triangles moving smoothly over the flat surface, punctuated by the occasional little lift into the air. Harry had his suspicions about what they were, but kept his thoughts to himself.

Anna led the way into a large white building, where there were the usual lockers, into which they placed their now redundant hoverboards and helmets. They passed into another room, which had large open double doors to the outside. Anna spoke briefly to a friendly woman, who disappeared through another set of large doors, only to return shortly after with a colleague, each guiding a hoverboard fitted with a mast and sail. It was as Harry had suspected.

Anna grinned at him. "Ever been windsurfing?" she asked.

"I can't say I have," answered Harry. While he liked the idea of giving the hoverboard windsurfing a go, he felt somewhat apprehensive about falling off.

He needn't have fretted though. The nice woman provided some brief instructions on how to control the board by angling the sail in the right direction. Harry felt more confident with the harness fitted round his waist securing him to his hover-sail, he now knew the correct term, and that the board was in safe mode. This ensured while he the windsurfer could not turn as sharply as he might wish, neither would he fall off, as both the board and the mast would always remain upright, and so prevent him from falling. Naturally Anna's hover-sail had its safe mode disabled, which she demonstrated in typical fashion, by using what little breeze there was inside to glide gracefully straight out through the double doors.

Tentatively Harry pushed his board outside. With the help of a guiding hand from the friendly woman he stepped on, pulled the boom in towards him, and instantly the strong breeze caught the sail and whisked him away.

"Bend your knees and lean back," cried out Anna, as she curved sedately around the back of him, before skimming neatly away across the large flat plain.

Harry did as instructed, tilting the sail forwards a little so he turned to follow behind the rapidly disappearing figure ahead of him. Feeling a little more confident, he attempted to bring the sail closer to the wind, only to find it wouldn't move any further; it had reached its safety limit.

"Ah well," he sighed to himself. "I may as well sit back and enjoy the ride."

He relaxed into a laidback position, the hover-sail happily holding him up, and realised he was beaming from ear to ear. Anna was far off in the distance, where she had joined some of the other windsurfers, who appeared to Harry to be executing stunts and tricks of some kind.

As he approached them he glanced down at the ground beneath the board to see a network of criss-crossed lines, which he assumed generated the electromagnetic field the hover-sails used to remain aloft.

"Come on Harry, it looks like you're up next."

Anna swept past the nose of his board, her black hair whipped across her face; Harry wondered how she could see. After she had passed, Harry realised with some concern that a small ramp lay directly in his path.

He was quite pleased with his line up, and thought he had executed his little hop off the top of the ramp rather stylishly. Harry however was less than impressed with his bouncy landing, the force of which jerked the boom out of his hands leaving him dangling backwards, with the harness round his waist his only salvation, preventing him from crashing to the ground. The sail swung round and flopped lazily in the wind, and the board slowed to a halt.

Harry pulled himself up on the harness, and looked round in embarrassment. A couple of the other windsurfers had watched his jump and whooped.

"Not bad for your first go," said one of them kindly. "Your line-up was excellent."

"Thanks," Harry responded, murmuring to himself, "Actually that part was sheer fluke."

There were several small humps in the vicinity of the first, and Harry soon acquired a reasonable standard, gaining a little more air each time he hit a jump. He was grateful for the built in safety design of his hover-sail, and progressed quite quickly onto the larger ramps Anna and the other windsurfers were using to perform quite spectacular aerial manoeuvers. Harry kept his own tricks to simple jumps, concentrating instead on increasing speed and amplitude, always with a mind on landing without embarrassing himself too much.

Anna would often sweep around behind him, ever careful not to steal the wind from Harry's sail, calling out useful tips and offering guidance on his stance or the position of his feet.

The exertion finally took its toll on Harry, and after a brief word with Anna, he returned slowly but smoothly to the rental building. Anna said she would join him shortly, once she had completed a few high speed runs.

As Harry approached the large open doors of the building, he saw the pleasant woman who had helped him onto the hover-sail talking to someone a little way inside the shadows of the doorway. Harry thought nothing of it, until too late he recognised the form of Rience. He resisted the desire to look back over his shoulder for Anna.

"Okay, play it nice and cool," he murmured to himself, as he brought the hover-sail to a halt in front of the doors.

"Hi Rience," he called out, waving at the man from the Authorities.

"Hello Harry, good to see you again," came the kindly reply.

Rience helped Harry guide the hover-sail into the building, where the woman took it from them and returned it to the store room at the back. Rience made polite conversation, asking Harry how he had got on with hover-sailing, hoping there weren't too many broken bones. Harry replied in kind, and decided to take the initiative.

"So, what brings you here?" he asked, as genuinely as he could.

"Oh you know, doing my rounds," answered Rience nonchalantly.

Harry had no idea what that meant, so pushed a little further.

"If it's Anna you're after, she shouldn't be too long," he offered. "She said she wanted to get in a couple of quick runs before finishing."

"Oh no, that's okay," replied Rience, darting a hasty glance through the doors, before fixing Harry with a steady look. "Actually, if anything, I could do with a brief word or two with you Harry."

Harry swallowed hard, but nodded all the same; this was exactly what he feared. "Of course," he answered, then in a flash of inspiration, "is it to do with Anna?"

The man from the Authorities looked at him in surprise.

Harry seized the moment and continued, "She told me all about her parents," he explained. "You probably won't know, but my own parents died when I was young. I think that may be why Anna and I get on so well, having that connection you see."

Harry felt justifiably proud of himself, wishing only that Anna was there to witness his little performance.

"Oh, is that right?" Clearly Harry had caught Rience off guard, and the confused man didn't know how to respond.

Harry ploughed on relentlessly. "She told me how you and Sorrel have been looking out for her, especially since she moved back into her own place by herself. I think she's much better off this way. You know, she's happier than when she lived with the other people who helped out after the accident. After all, from what I've heard, I don't think she made a particularly good houseguest." He laughed.

Rience appeared to relax a little. "So what have two been up to since you arrived here?" he asked, quickly adding. "By which I mean, what have you been doing?"

"Oh didn't Sorrel tell you? We've been trying to get the mini hoverboard track working again. Something seems to be interfering with the controls. That's about all really, besides going hoverboarding for real, and today hover-sailing. But I don't think you have anything to worry about. Anna seems to me to be quite happy."

"I suppose you're right," admitted Rience, who now appeared somewhat confused.

Harry smiled at him, as if waiting for him to say something else.

"Well, thank you Harry, I suppose I must be going now," said the man from the Authorities, glancing uneasily through the open doors, as a small triangular sail grew steadily larger as a hover-sail approached.

"Back to work now, is it?" asked Harry.

"Er yes, see you Harry."

"Bye, Rience," said Harry, shaking the man's hand the Tamarisk way, by gripping his wrist.

Rience hurried from the building, glancing once over his shoulder and giving Harry a quick nod, his eyes on the large open doors.

Chapter 19 – Back to Earth

"What are you grinning at?" asked Anna as she sailed in and jumped from her hover-sail. "That's the sort of smile which says, I'm feeling rather pleased with myself, and not the type anyone usually gets from their first time hover-sailing."

"You're too clever for own good, has anyone ever told you that?" Harry replied.

"Only you so far." Anna passed the hover-sail to a man who took it through to the back room. "Now don't change the subject, come on, out with it."

Harry shrugged his shoulders. "Your friend Rience was here, that's all."

"Oh really?" said Anna slowly, her voice full of suspicion, as she looked in the direction of the exit door. "You can tell me all about it in the car on the way home," adding, "by the way, how did you find the hover-sailing?"

"Great!" replied Harry.

The bubble-car whisked them back to Anna's house, returning the same way they had come, passing by the familiar vegetation covered dwellings, as Harry recounted his conversation with the man from the Authorities.

"Wow, Harry, you did fantastically well," declared Anna, as they entered her home.

"I thought so too," said Harry, conscious for once he hadn't needed to rely on Anna's quick thinking. "Hopefully the Authorities will leave us alone for a while."

"I'm sure they will," agreed Anna, nodding her head enthusiastically, closing the door behind them.

Harry felt quite tired, feeling all too much the long days and morning's physical exertion. After a light lunch he fell asleep in one of the soft chairs in Anna's living room, awaking about an hour later to find himself alone. He was not surprised, and after a satisfying yawn and stretch, joined Anna in the secret lab.

For the next two days they worked hard, and as Harry's understanding of the concepts of the wormhole technology improved, they were able to apply more and more of their knowledge to the practical workings of Anna's parents' prototype equipment. At times though it seemed for every step they took forward there followed two steps backwards, but they persevered and continued to make headway.

Despite their progress there was always that one elusive stubborn conundrum which refused to give up its solution, no matter how many different ways they attacked it. Anna in particular was becoming increasingly frustrated, until late one evening she unexpectedly let out a shriek of excitement.

"Don't tell me you've cracked it?" asked Harry, optimistically.

"You're right, I'm not about to, sorry," replied Anna, leaning back in her chair and placing her hands behind her head. "I was thinking about our upcoming trip back to Earth and something else came to me. It's a long shot, but Harry, do you have any of your parent's things in your house back home?"

"Um, not really," replied Harry dubiously. He rubbed at his chin thoughtfully adding, "There might be something in the attic though. Come to think of it, I do vaguely recall there being some boxes up there with their names on, but I don't remember seeing any bundles of paper tied with string, if that's what you're thinking of."

"But those boxes have got to be worth a look haven't they?"

"Sure, why not? We have nothing to lose, but you shouldn't raise your expectations too much."

"I know, but I have a good feeling about this," said Anna.

Harry pursed his lips; he wasn't so sure, but as usual kept his pessimistic thoughts to himself.

They had arranged to meet Sorrel at the terminal first thing on the day of the funeral for Harry's grandfather. Having worked late the night before, they were both quite tired, especially Harry, and the early start did little to help. The underground train had brought them to the terminal, stopping briefly at the station beneath the cloudscraper where Anna had her apartment.

"I thought you would prefer the scenic route on your arrival," Anna explained to Harry, when he questioned why they had travelled by bubble car on his first day.

There were few other passengers on the train, as most were heading for work, taking the train travelling in the opposite direction.

Sorrel had arrived ahead of them, and was waiting at the entrance to the space portal room. He bounced around joyfully when they joined him and together they went through to the check-in desks.

"You two look rather tired." Sorrel beamed at them. "Up late last night were we?"

"Yep, and the good news is, we got the hoverboard table working again," Anna answered. "You seem particularly cheerful this morning Sorrel," she observed.

"Well of course I am," he declared. "After all, this is my first visit to Earth."

"You haven't forgotten of course, that we're going to Harry's grandfather's funeral, have you?"

Sorrel became contrite. "No of course I haven't, I am sorry," he said turning to Harry, who managed to hide his emerging grin, as he recognised full well Anna's little game.

"It's okay," he said. "And we're only going for one day, a short day at that. Did you know we only have twenty four hours in a day on Earth?"

"Yes, I had heard." Sorrel nodded his head knowledgably, his brow furrowed in thought. "And is it true you have only one sun?" he said, looking rather worried.

"Yes, that's true as well." Harry laughed.

They checked in with Anna's friend, whom they had rushed past on their arrival a week earlier. She gave Sorrel a queer smile and shot Anna a questioning look, when the man from the Authorities was looking in the other direction.

"Gate thirteen," she said pleasantly. "Have a nice trip, although I hear the weather's not too good on the other side."

They thanked her, and made their way towards the portals, where there was a gentle murmur of excited chatter amongst the other travellers. Harry noted there was a rapidly shortening queue at door eight, where all the travellers walked through individually, one after the other. Anna explained that Harry need not hold her hand this time, as he would now have his own gate transponder.

"Along with your cloaking add-on," she stated, looking at Sorrel.

"Yes, yes, of course, I nearly forgot," he apologised, and reaching inside his jacket, he produced two small boxes which he clicked together. "Harry my friend, do you have your universal translator please?"

Harry took the neat device from his pocket, and gave it to Sorrel, who clipped it onto the new box. Beaming, he returned the upgraded assembly to Harry. "There you go my boy, you're good to go. You can now pass safely through the portals by yourself, and before we leave the hub on Earth, turn on the cloaking unit, and nobody else will be able to see you."

"How do I do that?" asked Harry, anxiously.

"Don't worry, I'll show you," said Anna gently. "I'll have to give you a lesson on how all of it works when we come back."

Harry looked again at the queue of passengers exiting through gate eight, noting they were enormously excited. He commented on it to Anna.

"The pleasure planet," was all she said by way of explanation.

They joined the back of the queue at their own gate, which included several rather good-looking people wearing sunglasses. Anna enlightened Harry, reminding him Earth's sun was much brighter than the twin suns of Tamarisk, and so shades were a sensible precaution.

"But your friend said the weather wasn't too good on the other side today, so do we need to protect our eyes?"

"No not really, but those people are probably pop stars."

Harry looked more closely, and thought the four lads with long hair immediately in front of him did look a bit familiar.

Anna continued, "Have you never wondered why the rich and famous are always wearing sunglasses?"

"I always thought they were all totally insecure," said Harry as he watched the boy band disappear one by one through the portal.

"I'm sure some probably are, but it's more often a clue as to where they've been. All Earth people have to come through Tamarisk so the Authorities can monitor them. Of course they nearly all go straight on to the Pleasure Planet anyway, and it's even darker there than on Tamarisk."

"Oh, but I thought it was only a few scientists who were allowed to travel by space portal."

The last of the boy band members vanished through gate number thirteen.

"And rather a lot of rich people as well," mused Anna. "Don't you find it funny how money can be allowed to bend the rules?" she added disapprovingly.

Sorrel interrupted their conversation in his usual excitable way. "Come on, it's our turn," he chirruped gleefully. "Anna, it's ladies first, so after you please."

"No, that's okay. Earth is Harry's home, so he can go ahead of me, and you can follow behind."

She pushed Harry gently ahead of her, and he looked straight at the gate and chuckled at the way Anna had taken control, refusing to let Sorrel dictate what they should do.

"Rebel," he muttered under his breath, but loud enough for Anna to hear, and marched confidently through portal number thirteen.

Chapter 20 – Cloaked

George looked up at Harry and gave him a friendly greeting.

"Welcome back Harry," he said. "Have you enjoyed your first week away from planet Earth?"

"Yes, thank you," he replied.

George beckoned Harry over to his desk, just in time as Anna appeared right where Harry had been standing only a few seconds earlier.

"Hi there George," Anna called out cheerfully.

"Hello Anna, always a pleasure."

Sorrel joined them as Harry looked around. The inside of the hub was no different to when they had last passed through the first time, but outside it was daylight, if somewhat grey and drizzly as Anna's friend had correctly advised them. What was different was the large crowd of people outside the stones, and most unsettling of all was they all appeared to be staring right at him. Harry realised of course that the hub's cloaking field rendered its occupants totally invisible, but it still felt a little unnerving to have so many pairs of eyes apparently fixed on them.

A little way beyond the hub, the members of the boy band were messing about, their cloaking devices hiding them from the crowd of visitors whom they dodged between. Harry noted they were all wearing dark sunglasses, despite there being no need for them, due to the overcast weather.

"So we'll see you later George," Anna was saying as Harry's attention came back to the hub.

"Righto Anna," replied the old man. "I hope everything goes okay today Harry."

"Thanks George," said Harry, unexpectedly feeling quite sad, and realising up to that time he hadn't thought too much about what the coming day was going to be like.

Anna showed Harry how to switch on his cloaking device, and accompanied by Sorrel, they passed through the shield of George's hub to the grassy area between the inner and outer stone rings, leaving the old man reclined in his chair reading a slightly crumpled copy of the local paper.

"Can we speak?" mouthed Harry.

"Yes, of course," replied Anna. "The cloaking devices hide our voices and any other sounds we might make. However, we must be careful not to bump into anybody. The transponder cloaking attachments aren't as powerful as the hub's, so uncloaked people will be able to feel you."

They walked cautiously in the direction the boy band had taken, passing by the outer ring of stones and stepping over the low wire, which kept the viewing public back from the prehistoric monument. Carefully and unlike the irresponsible boy band, they wound their way through the tourists, and passed through the gateway in the high fence, which Harry and Anna had clambered over on their last visit.

There was a sudden commotion, which made all the visitors turn and look. The members of the boy band had turned off their cloaking devices, appearing unexpectedly from behind a large black car with tinted windows. After signing a few autographs, they climbed into the car, which swept them away.

"They shouldn't have done that," said Sorrel critically.

"What was so wrong?" queried Harry.

"Nobody is allowed to appear in public this close to the stones," he answered sternly, his eyes narrowing, as he watched the departing vehicle. "It might arouse suspicions if famous people keep appearing here. They didn't even go and look at the stones, to make it seem like they were here for a reason."

"I'm sure they'll say it was a publicity stunt," Harry suggested sympathetically.

"I'm sure they will," agreed Sorrel. "Whatever they do though, when we get back I'm going to make sure it's their last trip off this world."

Harry was about to object, but saw the look in Sorrel's eyes, and a subtle shake of the head from Anna was enough to remind him not to trifle with the Authorities, however beguiling Sorrel might sometimes appear.

Anna attempted to change the mood. "Right, shall we work our way into town?" she suggested.

"What about the bike?" whispered Harry.

"It won't be there by now," replied Anna. Sorrel appeared to be lost in thought, as he gazed up the road. Anna continued quietly, "If we get the chance, we can always borrow a new one when we're in town."

"What do you mean 'borrow'," hissed Harry.

Anna winked at him mischievously, and he frowned his deep disapproval, at which Anna adopted her most angelic innocent look.

"There's a bus stop at the visitor's centre, where we can catch the tour coach back to town," said Anna.

"Nonsense," declared Sorrel, awaking from his reverie, and turning to face them. "Follow me, I have made arrangements."

In the far corner of the car park sensibly located behind the visitor centre, they found a minibus, also with tinted windows, beside which stood a man in a black suit, peaked cap and sunglasses. The side door was open and the three of them bundled into the vehicle, where they turned off their cloaking devices. The waiting driver clearly noticed their obvious presence, slid the door shut and climbed into the driver's seat. He removed his cap and glasses, and turned round to face them.

"Shall we go?" he asked, his eyes twinkling deviously.

It was Rience.

Chapter 21 – Social Issues

Harry and Anna laughed forcefully.

"Surprised you, didn't we?" roared Sorrel, slapping them both on the back. "I knew we would need to find a way into town, so what could be better than to ask my own boss to drive us there."

"Good one, Rience." Anna regained her composure quickly, while Harry tried to smile. He was worrying if they did find anything useful in his grandfather's attic, it would be difficult to get it back to Tamarisk if both Sorrel and Rience were tracking them. Clearly their assumption that Harry had put the Authorities off the scent when he last spoke to Rience was somewhat premature.

"It made sense really," explained Rience. "Sorrel has never been to Earth before, but I have, and I know the area quite well. I even learned to drive here in my youth."

Harry hadn't thought about that; nobody on Tamarisk had to drive themselves.

All of a sudden, Rience became quite earnest and looked intensely at Harry. "Harry, I want you to recognise we are your friends. I know The Authorities can seem a little austere, perhaps not quite as relaxed as the police on Earth, but I'm sure you'll come to appreciate things work pretty well on Tamarisk. Isn't that right Anna?"

"Of course," she agreed readily. "We're like one big happy family," she added.

"Alright, don't push it," said Rience, turning back to face the front.

He started the engine, and pulled smoothly away and out of the car park.

Harry exchanged a sympathetic look with Anna, then sat back and resigned himself to the ride into town. Things were not going quite as he had expected or hoped for. He had imagined the two of them having a similar sort of adventure to the one on their way to the Ring of Stones one week earlier. He grinned as he thought back to that wonderful carefree ride out of the city, which contrasted entirely with the sedate driving of Rience's, although Harry had to admit for someone from another planet, Rience's skills behind the wheel were impressive. He wondered how long the man from the Authorities had spent on Earth, to have become such a good driver.

Sorrel was looking out of the window, and up to the sky.

"Only the one sun," he murmured. "Absolutely remarkable."

Harry sniggered.

"Oh Harry, you don't know how lucky you are to live on Earth. Most star systems with habitable worlds are binary star systems, like you've seen with Tamarisk. When Earth finally gets to open up to the rest of the galaxy, it will be a popular destination. You lot only have to stop killing one another that's all."

Anna couldn't resist the opportunity and chipped in. "Yes Harry, if you could just do something about that please," she said with a straight face. "If it's world peace Sorrel wants, it's world peace Sorrel should get."

"Oh yeah, sure," replied Harry, unable to hold back a smirk. "I'm a bit busy I'm afraid, but how about tomorrow, will that do?"

"You two are always teasing me," complained the disgruntled man.

"Sorry Sorrel, it's Earth humour, we can't help it," replied Anna.

"Today is a serious day Anna," Sorrel said pedantically.

"I was trying not to think about it too much," Harry said softly. Coming back to Earth was an all too real return to reality for him. Whilst on Tamarisk, it had been relatively easy to forget about the death of his grandfather, and he knew he had been using the escapism and their work in the secret lab as a distraction. He looked across at Anna, who appeared to be wearing the same expression he assumed he had himself. Harry wondered if she was also thinking about the same things as him.

Rience drove into the city and dropped them off outside the front door to Harry's old house. It had only been a week or so, but the place didn't feel like home anymore. He took out his key and they entered, quietly closing the door behind them.

"It must feel good to be home Harry," suggested Sorrel.

"Yeah, I guess," he lied. "Have a look round if you like Sorrel, make yourself at home."

"Thank you Harry, you really are a most convivial host," Sorrel declared dramatically, and strolled off in the direction of the kitchen.

"I don't care about the house now," Harry said to Anna. "Couldn't I sell it and come and live with you?"

"Well, of course you can stay with me, for as long as you like, but you ought to retain your place in this world as well." Anna placed an affectionate arm around his shoulders, whispering, "After all, your parents might like a house to come back to, don't you think?"

Harry smiled, if somewhat forlornly. "Of course," he replied.

"Have faith, Harry."

"Let's get today over with first can we?"

Anna gave him a tight-lipped smile, and nodded. "I understand," she said, adding "all too well, unfortunately."

A sudden loud authoritative knock at the front door made them both jump. They laughed, as relief replaced the mixture of emotions they were feeling. Harry opened the door. A stony faced thin wrinkled old woman glared at him, and instinctively he knew she was from social services.

"Harry, is it?" she demanded.

"Yes," Harry replied politely, "and who may I ask might you be?" He attempted to present the same air of innocence Anna seemed to be so good at.

The woman pursed her lips tightly, took a deep breath, and let it out slowly. She had met plenty of insolent youths like this one before; they were all the same. She would play the game, and win, as she always did. She took on a patronising tone.

"My name is Gertrude and I, young man, am from the local authority social services. I'm quite surprised you didn't realise." She knew making him feel ignorant would be a good start.

"Oh, I do apologise, I've never had any reason to meet anybody like you before," Harry replied contritely.

That's more like it, thought Gertrude, although caught a little off guard. Harry appeared to be quite polite, and so maybe he was being truthful after all, even if the girl standing behind him was wearing a disrespectful smirk.

"Really, I thought perhaps you were a door to door salesman or something," said Harry.

Nope, she had been right the first time, thought Gertrude. Impudent, through and through.

"May I come in?" she said, stepping forward.

Harry was about to step aside to let the social services woman in, but felt Anna push up behind him, preventing any means of entering the house.

"I'm afraid it's Harry's grandfather's funeral," Anna informed the woman pompously. "We shan't be receiving any visitors today."

Harry's expression twisted into one of pain, as he attempted not to snigger.

"I am well aware of that, thank you young lady," replied Gertrude. She took Harry's contortions to be a symptom of his grief. "You have my deepest sympathy Harry," she said. "However I must insist, as I need to inform you of where you will be living after the funeral. I shall be escorting you myself."

Harry's stomach turned with fear, and his face went white, and even Anna looked somewhat vexed.

Gertrude knew she had them now. She kept the momentum going, "In addition, you must tell me where you've been for the last week."

Harry took a couple of quick breaths, as his heart raced; there was no way he was going anywhere with this woman.

"Well when you didn't turn up on the day my grandfather died, what was I supposed to do? Fortunately friends said they would look after me, so I have been staying with them ever since."

"Oh really, and these friends of yours, is this one of them?" Gertrude waved a pale white hand vaguely in Anna's direction.

"This is Anna. I've been staying at her parent's house," answered Harry. He wasn't lying after all.

"It's not right, these things have to be done officially. You can't go making these decisions for yourself."

"Oh really, perhaps we ought to involve your boss," suggested Anna, at which Gertrude's mouth fell open. "I'm sure he or she would love to hear your reasons for not meeting with Harry when you were meant to, and how Harry had to rely on his friends instead." Gertrude clasped her hand to her open mouth, and whimpered pathetically, as Anna surged on in her inimitable style. "After all, it's best if these things are done officially, isn't that what you said?"

The last Harry and Anna saw of the woman from social services was her disappearing hastily round the corner at the end of the street. They had watched in silence from the doorway, to make absolutely sure she had gone.

"Well, I think that's the last we'll see of her," said Anna, theatrically brushing off her hands.

"I sort of feel sorry for her," said Harry.

"Okay, well you can feel free to chase after her, and explain how it has all been a big misunderstanding, and you would much rather go with her," said Anna.

Harry pretended to ignore her.

"I think it's time to go in," he said, and closed the door.

Chapter 22 – A Grade A Grey Day

Harry sifted through the mail, which included several condolence cards, whilst Anna showed Sorrel round the house, explaining to the ever-inquisitive man how everything worked, from the toaster to the coal-fired stove in the living room. Harry opened a letter addressed to him from his Grandfather's solicitor, who was also a friend of the family. The letter explained how a trust fund had been set up for Harry, and he would receive the house and savings when he turned eighteen. Until that day he would be in the care of social services unless he could make other arrangements. Harry phoned the solicitor and explained how he had talked things over with a lady from social services, and he now lived with a close friend. The solicitor sounded quite relieved to hear Harry had found somewhere to stay.

Harry went up to his bedroom, and packed a bag with some of his clothes and a few personal things he wanted to take to back to Tamarisk. He changed out of his jeans and into smarter clothes, which he hoped were suitable for a funeral. After much deliberation he decided against wearing a tie, recalling his grandfather had never been one for formality, and would probably have scoffed at the idea, saying something like, 'You're not going for an interview.' Harry smiled and sat down on the edge of his bed and looked around.

His bedroom was the only room he had ever had, the house the only home he had ever known, until he had met Anna. With a lump forming in his throat, he remembered all of the good times he had experienced with his grandparents, and felt a sudden overwhelming appreciation for everything they had done for him. They had raised him, and done a pretty good job he thought to himself.

His tears fell freely as his emotions got the better of him.

When Harry came down from his room, on seeing his red eyes, Anna had asked if he was alright. He told her he was fine, and she gave him a friendly reassuring hug.

The three of them walked the short distance to the crematorium in silence, an aptly sombre grey mist hanging over the city. Harry considered it odd that Sorrel accompanied them, but decided it was better for appearance's sake to have an adult with them, especially if they bumped into Gertrude.

The funeral went quite well, Harry thought, and wasn't nearly as upsetting as he assumed it would be. He reasoned having cried earlier made it easier for him to cope. He smiled warmly at the other funeral-goers, as they greeted one another on arrival. There were only about twenty or so, of whom Harry recognised relatively few.

Harry and Anna sat at the front, along with the solicitor friend and the nurse who had looked after Harry's grandfather, while Sorrel seated himself inconspicuously at the back of the chapel. There were a couple of readings and some hymns Harry recognised from school assemblies.

When the service was over, soft music played as they went outside, where the mourners all filed past Harry, expressing their sympathy and saying, "Sorry for your loss." The men all gave his hand a firm shake and he received several tight squeezes from old ladies, some of whom he thought looked a bit familiar, but he struggled to put a name to any of them. Harry, touched by their sincerity, wondered if maybe they did know his grandfather quite well after all, and felt slightly guilty he had thought otherwise.

The last people to leave were the solicitor and the nurse, who both expressed genuine sorrow for Harry's loss, and questioned him on what he would be doing next. Harry put their minds at ease, introducing Anna and Sorrel, explaining he was in good hands and they need not worry.

The solicitor said he would be in touch again nearer Harry's eighteenth birthday, but if Harry needed any help with absolutely anything, to give him a call. He led away the weeping nurse, putting a comforting arm around her. Harry smiled as he watched them depart; he was fairly sure they both lived alone, and liked to think something good might come from such a sad day.

On their way home they picked up a light lunch, which they ate in near silence in the front room. Anna and Sorrel made polite conversation, considerately leaving Harry in quiet solitude. He was deep in thought, not for the reason they thought, but because he was desperately trying to think of a way of getting into the attic without arousing suspicion.

He let out a big sigh, and Anna and Sorrel looked at him sympathetically.

"I think I'd like a bit of time to myself," said Harry.

"Of course," they said in unison, their faces full of concern.

Harry went up to his bedroom, and pulled the door too.

As he changed, through the crack in his door he could hear the voices of the other two talking downstairs. He waited until he had some confidence Sorrel wasn't going to follow him, and slipped out of his room.

He reached the attic via the second flight of stairs, which he crept up carefully, slowly opening the creaky door at the top, and switched on the light. Fortunately it didn't take him long to locate his parents' old boxes, which were all labelled neatly with descriptions like, 'Harry's Baby Things', 'Holiday Mementoes', and 'Mum's Knitting Patterns'. As he searched, he disturbed some dust, and quickly managed to stifle a sneeze. There was only one box which didn't quite fit in with the well-ordered others, it being tucked away behind the cold water tank and having simply the word 'stuff' scribbled on the side.

Nervously, Harry peeled away the single strip of brown packing tape holding down the top two flaps. He opened up the box and his heart practically missed a beat, as inside he found a thin bundle of papers tied with the familiar string. He pulled them out and it took only a cursory glance for him to confirm they were exactly what he was after. At the top of the front sheet was the mysterious symbol, which had always baffled Anna. He resisted the urge to untie the goldmine of information he knew dwelt within and start reading straight away.

He paused momentarily at the attic door, and listened for the sound of Anna and Sorrel talking, but could hear nothing. It was far too quiet. Harry lifted up the front of his t-shirt and tucked the papers into the top of his jeans, pulled his t-shirt back down to cover them, confidently opened the door and turned off the light. There was no one on the landing below him, so he closed the attic door with a satisfying clunk, and descended the stairs, as normally as he could. Within two steps there was the sound of the toilet flushing in the bathroom, and Sorrel stepped out as Harry reached the bottom of the attic stairs.

"Oh sorry Harry," he apologised, as if he hadn't expected to see him. "I thought you were in your room." Sorrel looked pryingly up towards the attic.

"I was, but I wanted to look at a few old mementoes before we leave," he said, forcing out a little sob and a sniff. The dust from the attic probably helped.

"Oh of course Harry, I understand." The man from the Authorities patted Harry gently on the shoulder. "You take your time, there's no hurry."

The doorbell rang.

"Ah that must be Rience, back with us already," said Sorrel, not moving, his eyes drifting over Harry.

"I'll finish packing," said Harry, dashing into his room and closing the door behind him.

Hastily Harry removed the precious papers and slipped them to the bottom of his bag under the stiff insert, which gave his holdall a little strength, and sank wearily onto his bed. He took one last look round his room.

"You can't bring them back from the dead Anna." Rience's familiar voice floated up from the hallway, as Harry carried his bag out onto the landing, and pulled his bedroom door closed behind him.

"No, but while I'm alive, they live on in me, that's all I'm saying," argued Anna. "That's one thing which keeps me going. It's true I used to think there was no point to living anymore, but I'm over that. You lot don't need to worry about me or watch over me anymore. I am grateful, but truly I'm fine. And I have Harry now."

"Talk of the devil," said Harry from the top of the stairs.

"And he is sure to appear," completed Anna.

Harry descended the stairs and looked at Anna and the two men from the Authorities.

"I think I'm ready to go home now," he said.

Chapter 23 – Wake Up

Harry awoke late the next morning. Slightly disorientated at first, he realised he was in Anna's flat in the cloudscraper. He recalled little of their journey home from the terminal, having fallen asleep in the bubble-car. In fact he could barely remember getting into bed; he assumed Anna must have helped him.

Harry sat bolt upright, wide awake and panicking. He looked down at himself, and breathed a huge sigh of relief. He was wearing all his clothes, and even had his trainers on. For one terrible split second he imagined Anna had undressed him and put him to bed like his grandparents used to when he was little. He and Anna might well be good friends but there were limits, and clearly Anna had not stepped over that line, thankfully.

Showered and dressed in clean clothes, Harry found Anna watching some form of zero gravity football match on the wall-screen in the living room. She was doubled-up in hysterics at the disastrous game, as the heavily padded players bounced uncontrollably around in a large clear box, feebly attempting to control the oversized ball whenever it happened to come near them. All too frequently, the referee stopped the game when individuals and sometimes pairs of colliding players got themselves into a spin, at which point tethered marshals would quickly come to their rescue before the whirling team members lost consciousness.

Anna had been up for some time, and explained the short day on Earth and even shorter night on Tamarisk due to their arriving in the middle of the night had upset her body clock.

"It's infinitely worse than jet-lag," she explained. "Earth and Tamarisk have days of different lengths, so when we move between them, the time difference, which happens instantly of course, can be anything. One time I left Earth in the evening, only to arrive on Tamarisk immediately after second sun-up. I was exhausted by tea time. Of course if I was any good at planning, I'd have checked ahead and travelled on a more sensible day."

"But where would the fun be in that?"

"Exactly," replied Anna cheerfully, leaning back and contentedly putting her hands behind her head. A wisp of hair fell across her face, but she left it where it was, the hair appearing to be every bit as happy as its owner.

Harry helped himself to some breakfast, and re-joined Anna, who had turned off the insane game, and was waiting for him.

"You seemed pretty tired last night," said Anna.

Harry, his mouth full, nodded and grunted an acknowledgement.

"Too tired it would seem to even mention what you found in your attic?" she queried.

Harry grunted positively, and slapped his forehead. He had forgotten all about the papers. He put down his breakfast, and rushed back to his room, dug out the neatly tied bundle from his holdall and returned to the living room, tossing the newly acquired secrets across to Anna. He swallowed his food.

"Sorry Anna, yesterday was quite a day," he explained.

"That's okay, I know," she replied in understanding.

Anna looked down at the papers in her hand.

"I can't believe you found them," she said in amazement.

"We don't know what they are yet, or if they'll be of any use. I was lucky though, Sorrel nearly caught me."

"Oh I know. He unexpectedly got up and said he needed the bathroom. I couldn't do anything. I was sure he'd catch you out. How did you know he was there?"

"Because I couldn't hear you rabbiting on of course," Harry answered cheekily.

"I think I shall choose to ignore that remark," said Anna, her eyes twinkling as she turned her nose up at Harry, before returning her attention to the sheets in her hands.

Hungrily she untied the strings and leafed through the small pile of precious pages, her eyes darting back and forth all over the new material. Harry sat beside her and looked on whilst he finished his breakfast.

"This is good stuff Harry, outstanding," said Anna softly.

"Do you understand any of it?"

"Er no, not really, but I have a good feeling. Some of it seems to relate to what we have been working on though."

Harry sighed.

"Oh come on Harry, I keep telling you, you have to have faith," cajoled Anna.

"I know, I feel a bit down I suppose."

Anna dropped the papers on her lap, and looked up at Harry.

"You know, when we left your house on Earth and you said you were ready to go home, I think it was the nicest thing I've ever heard in my life. Did you really mean it?"

"Yes I did Anna," Harry replied sincerely. "I feel like the door on my old life has been closed, and you have opened a new one to my future."

"Thanks, and nicely put. But I think we need to shake you up a bit," said Anna, getting up from the sofa.

"Oh we do, do we?" Harry replied suspiciously.

Anna pushed the sofa, complete with him on it, back against the wall, closed the doors and turned to face the wall-screen.

"Windows out," she said clearly, and the windows tinted themselves, blocking out the daylight.

"Games on," said Anna, and the wall-screen leapt into life as the lights turned out, and a myriad of endless coloured ribbons danced on the screen, as the room filled with resonant music that swept around them.

Intrigued and motivated by the grand introduction, Harry stood beside Anna, waiting to see what would come next.

A list of names, of games Harry assumed, appeared on the screen.

"Fitness," called out Anna.

"Oh do we have to?" asked Harry in mock sulkiness.

"Trust me, you'll enjoy this," answered Anna. "Free run," she said, selecting the required option. Harry noted that also listed were choices such as cycling, swimming, rowing, skating, as well as other words he didn't recognise. Anna moved away and sat back on the sofa. As the running game start-up screen appeared, the other three walls, tinted window, floor and ceiling in the room all lit up and Harry found himself standing on a path in the middle of a jungle. All around him the animal and bird sounds of the rainforest enhanced the authenticity of the simulation.

"This is pretty amazing," said Harry in awe. "It feels so realistic, but don't you want to join in?"

"It's better as single player. Two or more people can run together if they want, but it's best to keep up, otherwise the wall-screen splits and it doesn't seem as real with the line down the centre."

"What do I do?"

"Have you ever been in a jungle before?"

"No."

"Go and explore," Anna guided him. "Walk on the spot and you'll start moving. The faster you tread, the quicker you'll move, and if you want to turn a bend, lean slightly to the left or right to do so."

Harry did as instructed, stepping lightly, and the images around him moved as accurately as if it was real.

"We have things on Earth a bit like this," he said, "but I think they have some way to go to match this."

Harry picked up his pace. The path ahead of him curved to the left, so he leaned over, only a little too far so he jogged headlong into a huge tree. The images shook, and Harry stumbled forwards. Anna sniggered.

"Oi," complained Harry, "it's my first go."

He leaned to the right and the pictures on the walls swung round until he was back on the path. He set off running again, slowing when he came to any bends, and he soon grasped the hang of leaning the required amount to steer without crashing.

Anna opened the panel in the armrest of the chair and punched in some commands. "This should make it more interesting," she said.

Ahead of Harry, the path forked. "Which way should I go?" he asked.

"Whichever way you want," came the reply.

He leaned to the right and followed the new path, which started to go uphill. After a few seconds he found he was having to put in more effort to maintain the same speed as before, and started to pant.

"This is deceptive," he gasped. "I know I'm only running on the spot, but it's harder work. My games console at home does the same thing in the cycling, but this takes it to a whole new level."

"Level up," cried out Anna. "Well you did say so, didn't you?"

The trail flattened off, and Harry veered round another bend to find a fallen tree lying across his path.

"Jump Harry, jump," cried out Anna.

He did so, but his hurdle was too early and he clipped the top of the tree, the wall-screens lurching so that first the ground rushed up to meet him, followed by the jungle canopy rolling downwards.

Momentarily disorientated, it was enough for Harry to lose his balance and he fell to his knees. As he raised himself back to his feet, he could hear Anna snorting behind him. He ignored her and set off once more.

He soon became competent at jumping obstacles, and was able to relax into the running, and even look around at the scenery as he passed it by, taking in the multitude of creatures scuttling, climbing and flying amongst the vegetation. The scenes changed, so sometimes the path would open out into a broad clearing where elephants and warthogs drank from waterholes, and next he would be plunged into darkness where he would run that much faster, the low growling noises from the undergrowth his incentive.

He found the experience exhilarating, as he plunged through shimmering waterfalls, and swung on jungle vines, totally immersed in the game and easily forgetting it was all an illusion.

After about an hour he stopped on the edge of a cliff and turned from the path he had been following to look out over the immense rainforest as it stretched as far as his eye could see.

"That was incredible," he said to Anna. "Thank you. I feel quite alive now."

"I thought you might," she replied happily. "Pause game."

"I feel shattered as well mind you," he chuckled, collapsing onto the sofa.

"It's easy to overdo it, but a fantastic way to keep fit. And what you have seen is only a small portion of the whole game."

"I could spend all day on this."

"It's very addictive, and the total immersion aspect of the artificial reality can be all consuming. Many people have become quite depressed on returning to their more mundane real lives."

"I can quite understand that. With the way things are going on Earth, I think we can expect to see the same."

Anna showed Harry the other game scenarios, flicking through parks, deserts, cities which she explained were great for free running, undersea worlds, moonscapes and alien worlds, both real and imaginary. She produced something not unlike an exercise bicycle, which worked as well as, but in place of running. She explained how fitness centres on Tamarisk were much like the gyms on Earth, but with more sophisticated set-ups using treadmill-like apparatus for a more authentic running experience, and smooth gliding machines for skating or cross-country skiing.

"It's a bit more interesting than running in front of a music video or the news like some do on Earth. However, I reckon this'll be the next big thing on Earth. The technology already exists in the consoles, the games simply need to catch up a bit," predicted Anna.

Chapter 24 – Home Again

"So are you ready to get back to work Harry?" Anna asked him after lunch.

They caught the swift white underground train and a bubble car back to Anna's home number two, Harry's bag their only piece of luggage, with the new notes from Earth tucked away discreetly at the bottom. Sensibly they avoided discussing the secret lab and their plans for the future, choosing instead to talk about Harry's activities that morning on the virtual reality machine. The news that Anna had the same device installed in her other house came as good news to Harry, even if he was a little put out by not having been shown it already.

"Sorry about that Harry, I guess I take that sort of thing for granted, and forgot to tell you about it," Anna explained it away casually, adding, "oh and by the way, did I also forget to mention this one comes with weapon accessories!"

Keen though they were to return to researching wormhole technology, they couldn't resist the first two hours home playing shoot'em up games on the walls, floor and ceiling of Anna's front room. As Anna selected one game after another, Harry soon came to appreciate there was a virtually limitless choice to the scenarios and styles of game available, which he found somewhat overwhelming.

"If we had this on Earth, nothing would get done, nobody would ever go out, we would all turn into troglodytes," declared Harry.

"Haven't you just described Earth's teenage population?" laughed Anna.

"Cheeky!" retorted Harry.

"Oh, sorry Harry," Anna exclaimed loudly, clasping a hand to her mouth.

"It's alright, I knew you were joking," replied Harry, startled by Anna's response.

Anna paused the game they were playing and frowned at Harry.

"No it's not that," she replied. "I completely forgot about your schooling."

"I hadn't," admitted Harry, "but I wasn't going to mention it."

Anna muttered to herself under her breath, her body tensed and her brow furrowed pensively.

"I'm surprised Rience hasn't been on to me about it, which makes me suspicious."

Harry looked at her earnestly.

Anna smiled and relaxed. "Don't worry, the school part is easy. You only have to average a couple of hours a day here at home using the virtual system, and complete a small test every ten days or so. You'll find it easy, especially the science stuff, and the rest is merely a case of repeating back what you have been taught."

"So why aren't you still doing school stuff?"

"Well, I would normally, but I passed all my exams last year, which was over two years early."

"Impressive."

"Thanks," replied Anna modestly.

"And now you just bum around," teased Harry.

"Yeah, well why not," said Anna. "I'll probably get a job when I'm twenty though."

"What will you do?"

"There's a planet where they're really keen on modding. You know, changing existing products to suit your own needs, or upgrading standard systems to something cooler. Well, there's a company that designs and manufactures modular cars, which people can upgrade themselves at home when they can afford it. In fact most people keep their car for life, starting off in their teens with something sensible, which isn't too powerful. As they get older and more experienced, they're allowed to make more modifications, if they can afford it. We have a house there, and I've already been offered a job if I want it."

"Sounds pretty neat," said Harry. "I'm not sure what I want to do when I'm older. But that sounds like it could be fun."

"I'll put in a good word for you," promised Anna, then returned to her original subject. "But I am worried about the Authorities. It's unlike them to be so quiet on a matter like this. They take education seriously here. I think it's how they keep everyone in line, by indoctrinating them through teaching one-way only."

"You make it all sound a little bit Orwellian. What do you mean?" asked Harry, somewhat bemused by Anna's apparent paranoia.

Anna noted Harry's scepticism. "I'm deadly serious Harry. I'm sure one of the other reasons for not allowing too many Earth people here is because of your propensity for rebelliousness."

"That would be our rebelliousness," stressed Harry. "You're a fine one to talk. I haven't forgotten where you came from originally, even if you seem to have done so. You may have moved to Tamarisk when you were young, yet it seems to me you can take the girl away from Earth, but you can't take Earth away from the girl."

"Yeah, fair enough, I suppose I do have a bit of an Earth streak in me," she admitted. "Speaking of Earth, I think the Chinese are similar to how it is here. They're all obsessed with teaching children lots of facts, and filling their heads so they can repeat back mathematical formulae by heart and so on. But there's no room left for any creative thinking. What use is all that knowledge if you've never been given the chance to think for yourself? It's what happens here on Tamarisk. I'm convinced that's why they employ scientists from Earth, because of your," Anna started to say but corrected herself, "sorry I mean our aptitude for free thinking."

"But it was here on Tamarisk they discovered wormholes, and look at the great things you have here," argued Harry. He went on to list all he had experienced since their arrival, while Anna sat and listened with a wry smile.

"Remember the wormhole discovery was a bit of an accident, and there have been plenty of changes since, many of which have come from other worlds. Waging war was what the people of Tamarisk were good at, and they invented some wonderful weapons they used to well-nigh destroy the planet."

"Well, you're the expert," accepted Harry, attempting to put an end to the conversation.

Anna ignored him and continued on regardless, causing Harry to grin.

"It can be quite frustrating at times. I wish the Authorities would allow people a little more liberty to think for themselves, and the freedom to question any mistakes."

"Like our parents' disappearances?" ventured Harry.

"Exactly," answered Anna. "When we bring them back, the Authorities will have to acknowledge some wrong doing."

"So are we going to bring down the government?"

"No, I think we'll settle for getting our parents back. Don't forget it's not all bad on Tamarisk. I must stop talking, I'm in danger of turning you into a rebel, even when there's nothing to rebel against."

"It must be the anti-establishmentarian in me," said Harry haughtily.

"So now who's using long words?"

"Oh, it was nothing really," said Harry with mock modesty.

"That's okay, I forgive you your floccinaucinihilipilification," she said sweetly, turned and strutted away to the kitchen, leaving Harry open-mouthed and struggling to voice any sort of a response.

Chapter 25 – The Solution

They worked hard over the next few days and increasingly, Anna was able to leave Harry to work on his own, turning her own attention to other areas. Harry noted she spent a great deal of time poring over maps and what looked like space charts.

Harry, for the most part, looked through the new pages they had retrieved from his grandparents' attic on Earth. The mysterious symbol appeared frequently and seemed to represent something entirely different to all they had worked on so far. On the one hand this confused Harry greatly, but on the other it made sense because there was an obvious gap in their understanding of the research material they had already looked at. If only he could connect the two! The best he had theorised so far was the symbol might be some sort of adjustment or offset, but for what he didn't know, and it was only a hunch. He ran the idea past Anna, who unsurprisingly, was encouraged by Harry's idea, but like him was unable to see how it could be applied in practise.

They often spent time discussing what they knew already, evolving new ideas and theories. They remained unable to work out how Harry's parents could have created their own wormholes, seemingly out of nowhere with minimal power, when the accepted science proved wormholes either required loads of electricity or needed a place of gravitational importance such as the Ring of Stones to work properly.

Over the next few days Anna became increasingly paranoid, mainly because she was unable to see anyone following them. Harry suggested that maybe the Authorities had finally accepted there was nothing suspicious going on, at which Anna merely grunted. He decided not to pursue the subject any further.

Every two or three days the friends would leave the house to visit a mall or to go hoverboarding or hover-sailing, and on one occasion they made use of one of the fitness centres Anna had mentioned, where Harry experienced virtual cycling and cross-country skiing.

"How is it all these games and sports are the Earth type?" he asked, following one particular session when they had played a downhill skiing game, which required them to crouch down to accelerate, lean to negotiate the bends, and leap up when they hit the jumps. They had also competed in a riotous six way snowboard cross race, which Anna had won, much to the chagrin of the other players. Naturally she dealt with the situation by tucking her uncooperative hair behind her ear, and sauntering off smugly, flatly refusing to a re-match.

"And more to the point, why don't we already have this on Earth?" continued Harry in frustration.

"I don't know," yawned Anna. "It must be down to a lack of imagination on the part of the software developers, because you already pretty much have the hardware.

"I can answer your first question though. You would probably be surprised to learn that prior to the invention of the space portals, sport hadn't been discovered on Tamarisk."

Harry stared at her in amazement.

"How is that even possible?"

"Before the War to End All Wars and the subsequent peace treaties, all anybody ever did was fight. The whole planet spent so much time waging war, they didn't have time to invent any sports!"

They had intended visiting one of the other simulator centres where the theme was flight, but found it closed for upgrading.

"No matter, it's getting dark anyway," said Anna. "We ought to be heading home."

Harry stopped dead in his tracks.

"Come on Harry, or we'll miss the next train," said Anna impatiently. She noted the wide eyed expression on Harry's face. "You've just thought of something, haven't you Harry? I think you've experienced your very own Eureka moment."

"You said it Anna," Harry beamed at her.

"I said what?"

"Dark matter!" replied Harry simply.

Anna was desperate to know what Harry meant by his statement, but unwilling to risk being overheard be anyone, she insisted they return home first. She found the journey unbearable as Harry sat with a satisfied and knowing smirk on his face. The more relaxed he appeared, the more frustrated Anna became, finally dragging him from the bubble car and into the house, and shoving him down towards the cellar.

"Right, that's enough torture for one lifetime," she declared as they crawled through the secret lab. "What does dark matter have to do with anything, and what is it anyway?"

"The Universe is filled with it," answered Harry. "But because it's dark, it's nearly impossible to see or detect. I watched a programme about it on Earth only a few weeks ago. Apparently most of the mass and energy of the Universe comes from stuff we can't see."

"And that's the so called dark matter?"

"Exactly! But what if it was everywhere, all around us, and pulling in all directions?"

"So what if it was?" queried Anna, completely puzzled by Harry's explanation.

"Well, that might explain why nobody has been able to detect it. Because the forces are all so balanced, they counteract one another."

"Okay," said Anna, dubiously. "Go on."

"So that just leaves the question, what actually is dark matter?"

"Right, that's the only question, is it Harry?"

Harry ignored Anna's sarcasm and continued. "If dark matter can't be seen but has lots of energy and mass, what else is there in the universe like that?"

"I don't know Harry. I think this is all a bit beyond me now," replied Anna, sighing and shaking her head. "The only thing I can think of is black holes, but they're huge, aren't they?"

"That's it though," said Harry encouragingly. "They are huge and usually lie at the centre of galaxies. But now consider if dark matter was in fact miniature black holes, too small to cause us any alarm, but black holes none the less, complete with the missing energy and mass."

"Harry, this is all a bit mind blowing. If you're right, do you think our parents realised it, and what does it have to do with wormholes? Are they related in some way?"

"I'm not sure if anybody else has thought of that, and I'm not even sure about it myself, to be honest," apologised Harry.

Anna looked somewhat dismayed.

"However," continued Harry, "before you lose all faith, I think it is the miniature black holes we are manipulating into becoming wormholes."

"Okay, I guess that would make sense," agreed Anna.

"You told me yourself wormholes were discovered by accident, and I'm guessing that to date there has been an element of pot luck in where the other end will open."

"That's quite true," said Anna, warming to the idea. "It's all kept fairly quiet, but I believe for each successful wormhole opened, there are many that ended in space, or in suns, or even a mile above or below ground."

"Not a pleasant thought," grimaced Harry.

"It's not so bad, they always send through a probe first. If those don't return at all, they don't even attempt a proper space jump."

Harry went on to explain how he reasoned that the peculiar troubling symbol adjusted their calculations, negating the influence of all visible matter, leaving only the dark matter, which Anna's parents' equipment could detect.

"That's where we've been going wrong," said Harry, looking at the set up in the secret lab. "We thought this was all about opening wormholes, but it's as much about detecting dark matter. It may even be the only fully functioning dark matter detector in the Universe."

"Wow," said Anna in amazement. "So what do we do next?"

"Actually, I think getting it to work should be fairly straightforward now we know what we're looking at. First thing in the morning, we'll give it a go."

"Are you joking?" snorted Anna incredulously.

"No, I'm being serious," replied Harry, feeling a bit injured by Anna's response.

"So am I, Harry," said Anna intently. "There's no way I'm waiting until tomorrow. Let's get this contraption working."

"Oh, okay," replied Harry.

Chapter 26 – Open Doors

They powered up the equipment, and armed with their new insight into the works of the apparatus soon recognised the previously unfathomable data for what it was. They disconnected much of the equipment previously used to amplify the power, reducing the controls to a single console. Anna's parents had selected one of two miniature black holes located in the secret lab and set up their equipment around it. The destination for the other end however remained a mystery, as that information had not been stored in the memory.

Harry and Anna reasoned that the probable cause for the disappearances of their parents had been due to using too much power to open the wormholes. If they had not realised they were dealing with black holes, their parents may not have expected there to have been so much readily available energy. Too much energy may have opened too large a wormhole, which in turn sucked them in, only for the fail safe to trigger and switch off the equipment, or in the case of Harry's parents, to perhaps cause an explosion as something overloaded.

After several hours setting up, checking and double-checking the system, they felt sufficiently confident to attempt the opening of a small wormhole. There were numerous destinations pre-programmed into the operating console and Anna selected the surface of a fairly benign planet within Tamarisk's own solar system. Harry placed a metal waste paper bin within the circle on the lab floor, which served as their test subject.

Retreating with the console to the relative safety of the first cellar room, they remotely controlled the dark matter wormhole generator via the house's own internal network. A camera in the secret lab provided them with a video feed, which they displayed on the wall separating the two rooms, so it appeared as if they were looking through the wall. Harry thought it was both impressive and a little weird, as it felt like they had acquired x-ray vision or as if a glass window had replaced the wall.

They both watched with bated breath as Anna gently brought on the power. Justifiably cautious, the minute incremental changes initially produced a negligible effect, but after several minutes Harry observed a subtle alteration of the air at the centre of the tripods.

"Look, there Anna, something's happening," he whispered.

Anna nodded silently, the only sound in the room a quiet satisfying whirr from the console. She continued to turn up the power, and gradually the distortion grew.

"How much power are you using?" Harry asked in a voice barely audible.

"Hardly anything," responded Anna just as quietly. "We're nearly there. This is incredible. The black hole is providing most of the energy. By the way, why are we whispering?"

"I don't know," whispered Harry in response.

They both giggled apprehensively.

After a few more minutes the distortion attained the same size as the waste bin which vanished abruptly, causing both Harry and Anna to jump.

"Quickly, reverse the wormhole direction," cried out Harry, rapidly coming to his senses.

Anna did as instructed, and magically the waste bin materialised as swiftly as it had disappeared. Reducing the power levels to a point deemed sufficiently safe, she turned off the device and turned to Harry. They both cheered and leapt for joy, hugging one another gleefully and leaping wildly about the lab. Once they had calmed down enough to function sensibly, they scrambled through the tunnel to the secret laboratory to inspect their test subject.

Without touching it, they crouched down and scrutinised the metal bin. It looked almost exactly as it had done prior to its intrepid space jump, except for a light frosting on the surface. Anna breathed warm air across the rim and it turned to vapour exactly as if she had exhaled outside on a cold day. She laughed excitedly.

"What does it mean?" asked Harry.

"The planet to which we sent our little friend here is at the edge of the solar system. There's barely any moisture there, and it's freezing cold. This is exactly how I would have expected the bin to return to us. So what it means is, the portal definitely works."

They sat back and relaxed, feeling both elated and exhausted at the same time, the frosted space travelling waste paper bin sitting patiently between them, as its covering of tiny ice crystals gently started to melt.

"So, do you still think it's time for bed Harry?" yawned Anna.

Harry chuckled. "No way. I will admit I never really thought we would get this to work though."

"Didn't I always tell you to have faith? I always knew you could do it," Anna smiled gently.

"I think it was a joint effort Anna," argued Harry. "And speaking of which, don't you think it's about time we retrieved your parents?"

"Do you definitely think we can do it?" asked Anna earnestly, getting to her feet.

"I do now," stated Harry.

"That's quite scary," said Anna softly. "I mean they've been gone for three years. And there is another challenge actually."

"What's that?"

"Well, we don't know where they went, do we? To recover them, if indeed they are stuck in limbo somewhere, we have to open the same wormhole they used, and we have no idea which one that is," said Anna solemnly, her shoulders sinking dejectedly. She leant back against the wall, and slid down it to sit on the hard laboratory floor. "They could have chosen anywhere in the galaxy, or even opened up somewhere randomly."

"I don't know about that," said Harry, shaking his head thoughtfully. "I can't imagine they would have picked just anywhere for their first attempt. Surely they would have chosen a safe destination."

"But where?"

"It would have to have been somewhere familiar. Perhaps somewhere they knew well, and a place from which they could return if there were problems," Harry mused, tapping his forehead with his knuckles. "Of course," he cried out ecstatically, looking up at Anna.

"The Ring of Stones," they chorused.

Chapter 27 – Back from the Brink

It didn't take long for the two friends to find the Ring of Stones' location listed in the console's memory, and the wormhole generator was soon up and running again, awaiting its next assignment. They removed from the circle their space jumping pioneer, the waste paper bin, and the three tripods were set to receive back the original explorers, Anna's parents.

"There's something else I've been thinking of," said Harry slowly as they crawled back through to the safety of the first lab.

"What's that Harry? Whatever it is, you're making it all sound rather ominous."

Harry chewed pensively on his lower lip. "The wormhole may affect not only space, but time as well."

"We know that. In fact aren't we relying on the fact?"

"Yes, but what if it doesn't work to our advantage?"

"What do you mean?"

"I mean, if your parents come back when we open the portal, they might be really old," he divulged reluctantly.

"That's right Harry. They may be too old. It may have been hundreds of years or even thousands for them," Anna concurred, much to Harry's surprise. "There is of course another possibility, which is the one I prefer to think of. To them, they may have been gone only a few minutes. Or even seconds."

"Let's hope you're right, but even so, they will find returning to see you three years older quite distressing."

"True, although they should recognise me, and it's by far and away the best result we can hope for."

"I agree," acknowledged Harry, and took a deep breath. "Alright Anna, go for it."

Nervously, she operated the console, slowly bringing a new wormhole into life, the tiny black hole effortlessly feeding it with all the energy it required to open and remain stable.

"Have you set the wormhole to travel in this direction?" asked Harry, anxiously.

"Good point," agreed Anna, correcting the controls. "How large do you think we need to make the portal?"

"I'm not sure. I guess until it's big enough for a person to fit through."

"I'll keep going until something happens," declared Anna.

"Okay," said Harry hesitantly. "But let's not overdo it. In fact, I don't think you'll be able to go beyond the tripods anyway."

They watched the wall-screen in silence as the distortion that was the wormhole portal expanded by degrees, quicker than before as Anna had adjusted the scale, more confident now they better understood the energy required. It was soon up to the same proportions as the waste bin, growing vigorously until it reached about the height of Harry, at which point Anna reduced the rate of expansion.

They held their breaths as the portal edged ever closer to the anticipated size of Anna's parents and, as with the waste bin, two figures appeared out of nowhere so instantly Harry and Anna once more jumped in shock.

Anna's parents appeared to be discussing something significant. They looked around the secret lab in surprise, frowning in confusion as if they had found themselves in an unfamiliar place.

"They look exactly the same," said Anna softly. "They haven't changed a bit."

"So no time has passed for them at all," added Harry with relief, turning toward Anna, but she had already dived into the cupboard and was scrambling frantically through the tunnel.

"Anna, what the devil do you think you're doing?" Harry heard her father cry out. "You know you're not allowed in here."

"And whatever have you done to your hair? Where are your lovely long curls?" contributed Anna's mother. "What's happened to your face? You look all wrong somehow?"

Harry remained in the first lab, watching the wall-screen as Anna rose to her feet in front of her parents, tears streaming down her cheeks.

Her father abruptly groaned despairingly.

"What is it?" asked her mother, looking from one to the other. "What's happened?"

Anna's father spoke tenderly. "Anna my dear, how long has it been?"

"Three whole years," she let out, and threw herself into their arms, sobbing desperately.

Chapter 28 – Reunion and Revelation

Anna and her parents found Harry sitting contentedly in the living room, drinking a cup of tea. He had turned off the wall-screen in the cellar and returned upstairs leaving them all to their emotional reunion. Alone on the sofa he was contemplating the repercussions of what had been achieved that evening. There was every chance in a short time he might meet the parents he never knew, and had always believed to be dead. It was quite unnerving and Harry wasn't sure he could ever be ready for such a meeting. They would be coming together as strangers, at least for him, but for his parents they would be returning to a life without their baby son. Instead of years raising their child, they would be facing a teenage boy they didn't know. Harry found it all quite disconcerting, even suffering a sense of guilt that by bringing them back it would be him robbing his own parents of the last thirteen years. He consoled himself by assuming they could go on to have more children, making him the much older brother. He liked the idea. Anna already felt like the sister he never had, but he had certainly not imagined the possibility he might one day have real siblings.

Harry put away his musings and put down his cup, and rose to his feet as Anna entered the room.

"Harry, I'd like to introduce you to my parents," she said happily. "Mum, Dad, this is Harry."

He felt quite overwhelmed by the affectionate embraces he received from them both. Anna's mother, clearly emotional, was unable to speak, so it was her father that spoke first.

"Of course, we knew you existed because we knew about your parents, but never considered the idea of asking for your help with our experiments. What you have achieved is incredible," he said in admiration.

"Well it was Anna who figured out most of it, and I've only been here for a short time," Harry explained, feeling rather embarrassed.

To make matters worse, Anna's tearful mother gave Harry another hug. Anna attempted a rescue.

"So anyway," she began, "I guess now it's time for us to recover Harry's parents, don't you think?"

"Yes of course," agreed her mother, wiping her eyes.

"But how can you be sure they didn't actually die in the accident, like the Authorities reported?" asked Harry.

"We can't be absolutely sure, but we saw the official report, which was top secret of course, and it did say the bodies of your parents were never found. Anyway, there's no time like the present. Shall we go back downstairs?"

"We need to be quick as well," said Anna's father gravely, as they descended the steps to the labs.

"Why's that?" queried Harry.

"Because your use of a wormhole will not have gone unnoticed. I suspect the Authorities will be on to us pretty quickly. They'll have detected the power surge, and want to know what's going on."

Anna turned on the wall-screen to display the secret lab, and grinned at her father. "But there won't have been any extra drain on the power grid. Harry realised the wormholes originate from mini black holes that supply all the energy we need. That's what your detector picks up. There's no need for the large amounts of electricity you were using."

"Most impressive Harry," complimented Anna's father. "Most impressive indeed."

"Thanks," mumbled Harry self-consciously.

"We thought we were on to something with the detectors, but assumed it was wormhole doors we were looking for."

"Well, you weren't exactly wrong," stated Harry. "There's one thing I don't understand though."

"Only the one Harry?" chuckled Anna's father, and Anna laughed.

"Oh, you're as bad as Anna," sighed Harry, shaking his head in mock exasperation. "I see where she gets it from now."

Anna's mother quickly came to his support. "You ignore them Harry. Now, please ask your question," she said.

"I was wondering how it was you were able to conduct your experiments in secret, when you must have been using so much power."

"Good point Harry," added Anna, nodding seriously. "We hadn't thought of that before."

Anna's mother smiled warmly. "Because it wasn't a secret. Rience has always known what we were doing. In fact it was his idea we carry on at home. The Authorities were happy to turn a blind eye to our experiments."

Harry and Anna gulped at the same time, and turned in horror to face one another, both fearful of the significance of this latest revelation.

"What's the matter?" asked Anna's father, seeing their concern. "Actually, I'm surprised he's not here, neither him nor Sorrel."

"But they don't know anything about what we're doing," answered Anna in confusion. "They told me you had both died in an accident at work. Why would they say that? When I first returned home, the door to the secret lab was closed. It looked undisturbed."

"They must have tidied up afterwards," suggested Anna's father.

"They were covering their tracks," interjected Harry bluntly.

Anna's mother shook her head gravely. "I don't think the Authorities know anything about our research, only Rience and Sorrel do. They've been using us for their own personal gain, but to what ends I do not know. And I'm sure they'll know you've succeeded now in opening a portal, there are other less official ways of detecting open wormholes than purely looking for power surges. I think all our lives may now be in danger."

Chapter 29 – Escape

"We have to get word to Emma," said Anna's father. "She could help us."

"The nice lady at the Authorities," Anna reminded Harry. "The one I stayed with, but didn't believe my theories. I'd love to see the look on her face when she sees Mum and Dad."

"You shall my dear," promised Anna's mother. "As soon as we have rescued Harry's parents we'll call her, but we must hurry. We have yet another problem though. Harry's parents were trying to travel from their old laboratory at our workplace to the Ring of Stones on Earth, but that lab has been dismantled. We daren't risk travelling there, as we don't even know what's in its place."

"But we don't have to actually go through the wormhole. All we have to do is convince George to open a portal to the lab, with the direction set from Tamarisk to Earth, and Harry's parents should come through, as you two did."

Harry whimpered, and put his hand to his head. "You mean to say, that's all anybody ever needed to do, to get my parents back."

"Sorry Harry, but yes, I think we do know that now," sympathised Anna. "They could have been brought back straight away thirteen years ago, if anybody had ever thought to try it."

Anna's parents apologised profusely. "We didn't know, although there were rumours. We assumed they had died as well, because that's what Rience told us. It's only because of what you have achieved in getting us back that has made us reconsider the official report."

"Right, enough talk," said Anna abruptly, startling them all. She turned on the console, which was already set for the Ring of Stones. "I marked the portal size when you came through, so we can open the wormhole quickly now with a pre-set power level."

"You are a clever girl," said her father proudly.

Anna looked slightly embarrassed as she leaned forward and started the sequence to create the wormhole. Right on cue, Anna's hair fell across her face, which her mother reached for and tucked behind Anna's ear, where remarkably it stayed.

"You look good with your hair short," her mother murmured approvingly.

"Okay, it's ready," said Anna, excitedly. "Now, who's going?"

"I will," said her father. "Poor old George will have the shock of his life, but I should be able to convince him to open a new wormhole."

After a hurried goodbye, he turned to crawl into the cupboard. "Okay here we go," he said.

Suddenly they were plunged into darkness as the lights and screens turned off. They all gasped with shock, before relaxing a little as tiny emergency lights switched on automatically.

"Is it a power cut?" asked Harry.

"Oh no, we have to get out of here," said Anna's mother in panic. "They're on to us."

"How do you know?"

"We never get power cuts on Tamarisk," explained Anna. "If anything there's sometimes too much energy to go round, despite the cloudscrapers using as much as they do. Rience or Sorrel must have shut down the power to this whole area."

"So, what do we do now?"

"We can't let them catch Mum and Dad, or us. We need to find somewhere with power."

Anna's father spoke. "The flat has its own backup, which might be enough to power the equipment, and seeing as you've made it all nice and portable we could take it there by bubble car and train."

"Good idea Dad," complimented Anna. She and Harry crawled through to the secret lab to retrieve the three tripods and their cables, whilst Anna's parents disconnected the console and packed it into a suitable rucksack.

They left the cellar and found another pack for the tripods, following which Anna used her transponder to request a bubble car. They waited uneasily by the front door. Through the glass, they could see that only in the distance were there any lights, and they could hear some of their neighbours outside talking in confused voices.

"Rience has gone too far," said Anna's mother crossly. "He can't possibly hope to get away with this."

"The bubble car's here," cried out Harry.

"That was quick," said Anna's father. "Services have certainly improved while we've been gone." He reached to open the door, but Anna put her hand on his, preventing him from doing so.

"Wait, things haven't improved that much. The bubble car was far too quick."

To their dismay, the gull-wing door opened, and by the light from within were silhouetted the sinister forms of two men.

"It's them, we were too slow," grumbled Harry.

"No way," said Anna defiantly. "I lost my parents once because of them, and I am not about to let those two do anything to them again. Quick, everyone, get to the back room."

They followed obediently, as Anna slipped on one of the packs, motioning for Harry to do likewise. Harry had not been in the back room before, having assumed correctly it was the bedroom of Anna's parents.

"What have you got in mind my dear?" asked Anna's mother.

"I have a plan. You might even say I planned for this eventuality. I want no arguments from anyone," she commanded, much to the amusement of all. "If this is to work, you must do as I instruct."

"Yes, of course dear, whatever you say," replied her mother.

"And absolutely no patronising!" continued Anna.

"Certainly not my love, we wouldn't dream of it."

Anna turned serious again and quickly explained her strategy, to which they all agreed, despite some worrying gaps that required their faith.

There was a loud knock at the front door, and the birdcall bell sounded.

"You'll need a bit more information before we go our separate ways," said Anna's father. "Firstly I need to tell you the coordinates of the old laboratory. Secondly there's something you should know about George so he believes your story."

He passed on the details, before they hugged one another tightly.

A loud voice called from outside. "Anna, it's Rience, please open up, we need to talk to you both."

Anna's parents quietly opened the bedroom window and climbed out. Carefully, they sneaked across to the hedge that separated their garden from next door's and proceeded to make as much noise as possible while attempting to climb through.

Harry and Anna meanwhile had crept back towards the front door, where they observed the men from the Authorities running off towards the unsubtle commotion at the rear of the building. "Quickly Rience, they're trying to escape," they heard Sorrel panic.

Their escape route cleared, Harry and Anna legged it to the bubble car and dived in, swiftly closing the door behind them. Anna punched in a new destination and their commandeered escape pod launched into the darkness as Rience reappeared, shouting over his shoulder to Sorrel. All Harry could make out were the words 'diversion' and 'kids', and he grinned at Anna as the first part of her plan succeeded.

"Don't relax yet," Anna warned him. "We still have a long way to go."

"I know," replied Harry, laughing as adrenalin started to flow through his body.

"But you have to admit, this is great fun," said Anna, but their merriments were short-lived.

As their bubble car joined one of the main routes, another one travelling in the opposite direction turned up the road to Anna's house.

"It's the one I ordered for us," moaned Anna. "I've inadvertently provided them with the means to come after us."

Chapter 30 – Flight through the Dark

"Can the Authorities stop our bubble car?" asked Harry, as they noticed the lights in all the buildings around them switch back on.

"I'm quite sure the real Authorities could, but Rience and Sorrel seem to be working independently. Cutting the power, even for a short time, will already have aroused suspicion amongst their colleagues. Like Mum said, they can't possibly think they'll get away with this."

Anna's mouth opened in a huge broad smile.

"What is it?" enquired Harry.

She put her hands behind her head and leaned back. "Talking about Mum like that, now they're back. It's such a good feeling. Oh Harry, I'm excited for you. You can't imagine what it's like."

Before Harry could tell Anna how he felt, a familiar voice sounded from a speaker in the bubble car.

"Anna, Harry, hi it's Sorrel. Listen, this has all been a huge misunderstanding. We've always known about the secret lab. When your parents disappeared Anna, we arrived to find the hidden door in the cupboard wide open, and them gone. We closed the door to the lab and let you carry on in the hope you would figure it all out, and I think you nearly have done. We want to help. We want this for everyone, truly we do."

"I don't believe a word of it," Anna said to Harry. "It's okay, they can't hear us."

Sorrel continued in his overly-friendly chatty way, "Look, we know you're heading for the station at the mall, and there isn't another train for a good fifteen minutes at least, so when you arrive, wait for us and we can all have a good talk about it. I'm sure we'll have a few larks as well, like always."

"Larks, I'll give him larks, who does he think he is now, Joe Gargery? Anyway, ignore him," instructed Anna. "There's something stored at the mall that we need."

"There's no need to run away. We don't care about your friends back at the house. All we want is to look at what you have in your bags."

"They know we have the equipment with us," said Harry worriedly.

Anna nodded soberly. "But they don't know about Mum and Dad. That gives us some advantage."

Five minutes later they arrived at the shopping mall above the station. They leapt from the bubble car, startling an old couple exiting the building. Harry called out an apology as he followed Anna to a locker room a short distance inside.

"Harry, do you remember I told you about the speedboards they have on the pleasure planet."

"Yes, but is this really the time?" sighed Harry.

"Well, they're illegal on Tamarisk."

"Okay, so what's your point?"

They stopped at a locker and Anna opened the door to reveal two impressive looking oversized hoverboards, which Harry recognised from a recent programme as the speedboards used on the pleasure planet.

"These should give us the edge over Rience and Sorrel," Anna declared proudly.

Harry couldn't resist the opportunity. "What, no go faster stripes down the sides?"

"Some people are never happy." Anna grinned, passing Harry a helmet, and strapping one on herself.

"Where's the nearest blue line?"

They picked up their boards and tucked them under their arms.

"This way," said Anna, heading towards the lifts. "Well, sort of, anyway," she added mysteriously.

They joined a small group of lads who looked too young to be out so late, and caught one of the lifts down to the station.

Harry and Anna stood quietly, resting their hoverboards upright on their feet, failing totally to look as natural as possible, as the boys gaped at them.

"How did you come by these?" whispered Harry, giving up his vain attempt to appear casual.

"Don't ask, I wouldn't want to get you into trouble."

"Of course, there's no chance of that happening. And you have them stored at the mall because…?"

"It's near the only place they'll work."

"Oh," said Harry in confusion.

They exited the lift ahead of the boys, Harry following Anna as she raced towards the station platform, their backpacks containing the precious wormhole generator gear bouncing uncomfortably on their backs.

"Harry, these boards don't work on the normal hoverboard routes, because the field isn't strong enough to generate enough lift." They stopped running and Anna turned towards the platform. "Have you ever given any consideration to why the trains are so smooth?"

"Special frictionless Tamariskian bearings?"

"No, it's because they don't have wheels."

"But there are tracks, I've seen them."

"The trains are hover trains Harry! The wheels aren't hidden away, they aren't there at all. The tracks you can see generate the electromagnetic field on which the trains float."

Harry started to feel numb as he realised what Anna was suggesting, but the adrenalin now coursed through his body in readiness for the flight to come.

There were already a few people waiting for the next train, who initially had watched with bemusement, as Harry and Anna hurried past them. Their faces changed however, as they watched Harry and Anna strap on the boards, and as Anna jumped down onto the track they started to shout warnings.

"Quick Harry. These people will have never seen anything quite like this before." Anna bounced over to the second power line.

"They're not the only ones," muttered Harry, his heart pounding in his ears as he jumped off the perfectly safe platform to float effortlessly on the invisible field generated by the first power line.

Over the sound of his beating heart, there was no gentle hum from his board this time, but a purposeful growl, which more than hinted at the power he could expect to come from his speedboard.

Anna set off quickly, as a shout came from behind them. Harry momentarily caught sight of Rience and Sorrel running onto the platform, before moving directly to the top of the field where he accelerated away at such a rate he found it difficult to lean forward.

"Oh we're both going to die," cried Harry, as he plunged into the darkness of the tunnel.

A light appeared ahead and to the right of him, as Anna turned on a helmet mounted torch.

"Press the button on your strap," she called out.

Harry did as instructed and illuminated the track ahead of him, not that there was much to see beyond the gentle curve of the tunnel and the parallel power lines on the ground.

"Faster Harry," yelled Anna, leaning forward. "We need to stay ahead of the next train."

"But they'll stop it, won't they?" Harry shouted back, as he dropped forward into a neat tucked position and caught up with Anna.

"I doubt it very much. If Rience and Sorrel realise what we're doing, they'll be keen to catch up."

They rode side by side, at a speed Harry found both terrifying and exhilarating at the same time. The wind stung his eyes, making them water.

Anna glanced across at him, wiping at her own tear filled eyes. "Next time we'll bring glasses," she yelled over the noise of the wind and the speedboards. "Should have thought of that really?"

"What do you mean, next time?" replied Harry, laughing in spite of himself.

It felt like the bike ride all over again. Despite being able to go in only one direction the thrill he was experiencing left him feeling profoundly liberated. Anna whooped loudly, evidently experiencing the same excitement as Harry.

"Faster Harry," she cried out again.

Harry watched as she leaned even further forward, crouching down into a tighter ball, her head craning forward, and her arms tucked neatly behind, creating as streamlined a position as possible, her black hair whipped back over her forehead. There was no chance of it falling in Anna's face, as her refined boarding technique accelerated her to new limits.

Harry sensed something behind him, and could hear the sound of what could only be the pursuing train. Highly motivated, he emulated Anna's stance, and gradually caught up with her.

They no longer chatted, as the situation became more serious, instead concentrating fully on maintaining their momentum, desperate to remain ahead of the rapidly advancing train. They both breathed a huge sigh of relief as ahead they saw a small glow from the lights of the next station.

There was a stunned silence from the late night waiting passengers on the platform as Harry and Anna rocketed past, some of whom only heard the noise of their passing speedboards, and others who convinced themselves they had imagined the scene altogether.

The station provided Harry and Anna with another opportunity to put some distance between them and the train, as it stopped to drop off and collect more passengers. They knew of course that Rience and Sorrel must be on board, in their now relentless pursuit of Harry and Anna.

Harry noted there were regular small doorways in the sides of the tunnel, which he assumed were for general maintenance purposes. It was close to one such opening that they almost collided with a works team patching up a damaged section of the tunnel wall. The three workers were on Anna's side, and to Harry's and their amazement she managed to slow enough, and leap across to Harry's power line, sailing over their heads as two of them ducked and the third dived for the nearest exit.

Anna contorted in pain as her body wrenched itself, and Harry started to slow down.

"No, keep going," she cried out. "I'm alright, there's nothing broken."

Harry could see she told the truth, and pushed back up to full speed, sensing Anna doing the same behind him. In tandem they ploughed on through the darkness, their little head torches lighting the way as they carved round the bends of the meandering tunnel.

Soon after, they recognised the light of their stop, reaching it comfortably ahead of the train. Harry shouted for joy, as they began their deceleration into the station, easing back and slipping slowly down off the apex of the magnetic field.

"I believe this is where we get off," shouted Anna gleefully, following Harry as he executed a neat little hop onto the platform, before sliding to a stylish halt in front of an amazed onlooker. Anna bumped gently into the back of Harry, and they collapsed to the ground, narrowly avoiding a collision with the somewhat mystified man who, not knowing what else to do, helped to disentangle and pull them back up onto their feet.

"I don't believe it, I'm still in one piece," exclaimed Harry.

Laughing with relief, they thanked the kind man, and unstrapped their boards and helmets, which they discarded as redundant excess baggage, and ran for the lift, with the disquieting soft swish of the trailing train arriving behind them.

Chapter 31 – Sky High Portal

They reached the apartment well ahead of the two men from the Authorities. As Anna opened the door, the lights in the building dimmed momentarily, a clear sign the power to the building had been cut. Anna laughed, confident in the knowledge not only did the entire building have a backup system, but the flat itself also had enough reserves for them to effortlessly drive the wormhole generator.

Once they were safely inside the flat, Anna locked the controls to the door, and dragged a chair in front of it. Meanwhile Harry removed the three tripods from his pack and set them up in the centre of the living room, the now familiar gun-like equipment he had joked about the first time he entered the secret lab positioned crudely in the centre of the room. Anna joined him and connected the console to the cables trailing from the tripods, connected the power, and turned on the equipment. She checked the readings and quickly discovered there were no black holes within range.

Hastily, Harry moved the tripods, positioning them to one end of the room, only to be similarly disappointed. He shifted them to the opposite end of the room, and again Anna had to report negative findings.

"What do we do?" Harry cried out in frustration.

To add insult to injury loud hammering on the door to the apartment panicked them as it announced the arrival of Rience and Sorrel.

"Quickly, try the kitchen," wailed Anna, disconnecting the power lead and snatching up the console.

Frantically, Harry grappled with the tripods, and stumbled along behind Anna, dragging the straggling cables across the floor as they moved through to the adjoining room. Rience's familiar voice shouted threateningly through the front door, accompanied by cursing from Sorrel as he struggled to override the security system preventing them from entering.

With the wormhole generator set up once more, Anna let out a triumphant cry as finally the activated console detected the highly desired miniature black hole they required to generate a wormhole. Quickly, Anna started the finely tuned process, stimulating the wormhole and promptly opening the portal that would transport them to Earth.

"You first Harry," called out Anna gleefully, at the sound of the front door clicking open, and the joyful cry of satisfaction from Sorrel.

"Fix it to turn off after you pass through," cried Harry as he leapt through the portal.

Anna set the control, and dived after Harry, giggling as she heard Rience and Sorrel falling over the chair she had placed behind the door. The men from the Authorities appeared in the kitchen doorway in time to witness Anna's feet vanishing into the wormhole and the portal closing behind her.

Chapter 32 – The Ring of Stones

George was napping peacefully in his hub, when the unexpected arrival of Harry followed by Anna sprawling on the ground in front of him caused him to leap to his feet in astonishment. At first, he assumed he must have missed a scheduled trip or the system had not alerted him to the imminent arrival of these new travellers, but a quick assessment of his controls showed everything to be in order.

Harry was the first on his feet. "Hello George," he said, his face beaming. He looked around and noted it was dark outside.

Anna stood up beside him. "George," she cried, "it's so good to see you."

"I assume you have a good explanation for this young lady," George demanded of Anna, glaring distrustfully from one to the other.

Anna grinned, "But of course we do George. We have our own wormhole generator."

"I don't believe you."

"Oh I'm sorry, haven't you heard? They're all the rage now on Tamarisk. Soon everyone will have one, and you'll be able to take that retirement I know you want so dearly."

Anna was back to her usual self, and Harry knew they were safe, for a while at least. With the portal closed, the only way now for Rience or Sorrel to catch them was to use an official wormhole and even so, they weren't to know for sure where Harry and Anna had gone.

Poor George looked pleadingly at Harry. "Please tell me what on Earth is going on."

Harry laughed. "Thanks George, 'what on Earth' has a nice ring to it."

Anna spoke seriously. "George, do you trust me?"

"No I blinking well don't," he replied in exasperation. "I know what you Earth types are like, disregarding rules and always trying to buck the system. Why can't you do what you're told and fall into line with the rest of us."

Anna smiled knowingly, and narrowed her eyes saying, "But I know you came from Earth as well George."

"It's not possible, nobody knows that," he argued defensively, quickly adding, "and anyway, it's just not true."

"My parents told me George," Anna continued slowly.

"And you decided to wait until now to mention it?" he responded suspiciously.

"No, they told me earlier tonight. They're back, you see," said Anna earnestly. "George, you know I wouldn't lie about something like that, would I? Dad said we could rely on you."

George sat back in his chair, shaking his head as he tried to absorb what Anna was telling him. "I think you two need to explain to me exactly what you have been getting yourselves into, and please do so in a language I can understand."

Between them, the two friends recounted the entire story, from Anna's initial trips to Earth in search of Harry and her enrolment at his school, through to their investigations on Tamarisk, and their ultimate success with the wormhole generator, which had brought them back to George's hub.

George listened intently in silence, sometimes scratching at his furrowed brow, often frowning at their antics, in particular their escape on the speedboards, and appearing quite glazed when Harry explained his dark matter theory.

When they had finished, Harry and Anna looked at one another satisfactorily, while George reclined in his chair, mulling over their story.

Eventually, he rubbed his rough-skinned chin with one hand, before asking in a measured voice, "So what do you require from me?"

"We want you to help us recover Harry's parents," answered Anna.

"Okay, so how do we do that?"

"We need you to open a new wormhole to these co-ordinates on Tamarisk," explained Anna, scribbling down two sets of numbers onto a notepad on George's desk.

"It's against the rules Anna, you know that," answered the old man, shaking his head as he picked up the piece of paper.

"So will you do it?" Harry asked optimistically.

George nodded his head ever so slightly, "Of course I will Harry."

Anna ran round the desk and kissed the surprised man on the top of his head. "Thank you George. My parents were absolutely right about you."

Masking his embarrassment, George started the process to open a new wormhole. "Now it needs to be in this direction of course," he murmured.

"I think he knows what he's doing," whispered Harry.

"Fortunately, there aren't any trips booked for another hour, so we're safe to open a wormhole," he explained. "We always get a few visitors for sunrise."

He entered the new coordinates into the system, as portal number two lit up the stones in yellow, and Harry and Anna stepped back eagerly, allowing plenty of space for the anticipated arrivals.

"This will probably cost me my job, you realise," said George apprehensively.

"Thanks George, I know you're taking a big risk," replied Harry.

"When the Authorities realise what I've done they'll descend on us pretty quickly. They may even shut down the hub." He glanced from the now open portal to the display in front of him. "I'm detecting two life signs," he cried out in surprise. "They're dim, but growing stronger, and should arrive any time…"

Before them appeared a man and a woman, outlined by the yellow portal and stones behind them.

"Any time now," Harry completed the sentence quietly.

The couple before him looked too young, until he remembered his parents were only in their early twenties at the time of the accident. He thought back to the only photograph on display in his grandparents' house, and realised the unfamiliar setting and shock must have confused and numbed him, because against all his uncertainty, before him now stood his mother and father.

They smiled at him, and Anna, and George, as they looked around, appearing only slightly confused. George was the first to move, leaping professionally into action, rushing forward to greet them.

"It's alright, we have a protocol for this," he said. "Not that I ever thought I'd have to implement it."

Slowly and sympathetically, George explained to the new arrivals the nature of their return at which they expressed considerable bewilderment.

"But we only just left a few seconds ago," argued the man, glancing around him, desperately looking for some evidence to support his statement.

"Actually you've been gone for some time I'm afraid. It's been twelve years," explained George. "There was an explosion at your lab. You have been presumed dead all this time."

"Oh no, our little baby boy," cried the woman, clasping her hands to her mouth, as tears welled in her eyes. "Do you know what's happened to our son? Is he alright?"

George and Anna turned and looked at Harry, and the eyes of his parents followed until they rested unknowingly on their son.

"There's no need for you to worry," Harry reassured them, "because I'm absolutely fine."

Now sobbing inconsolably, Harry's mother walked across the gap between them and placed her hands on his cheeks, and looked deeply into his eyes.

"I don't believe it," she whimpered. "It is you. You're my son." She flung her arms around him and squeezed him tightly to her body, resting her nose on his head. "Oh, I am so sorry, whatever have we done?"

Harry's father joined them, and Anna and George retired to the other side of the desk to allow the reunited family what little privacy they could.

Through many tears, Harry and his parents started out on the tentative first steps of an emotional journey, which would encompass the last decade, including the harsh news that his father's parents had passed away during the intervening years.

George's soft voice distracted them all. "There's a wormhole opening," he said bleakly. "Now we're for it. The Authorities are on their way."

Portal number three lit up, and Harry couldn't help but smile wryly as he recognised the familiar site of the stone doorway from his first space jump to Tamarisk. Abruptly, a woman from the Authorities appeared in the empty space, and walked briskly forward to allow others to follow. Desperately, Harry hoped they would be able to explain to the Authorities what had transpired, but had Rience and Sorrel already told a story of their own? Surely the reappearance of his and Anna's parents would be enough to convince anyone of the truth.

"Emma!" called out Anna, startling Harry from his thoughts, as she hurried past him.

"Hello Anna," beamed the woman from the Authorities, opening her arms to hug her. "You have been on an adventure haven't you my girl?"

Behind Emma, Anna's mother arrived through the portal trailed closely by her father.

"Reunited again," laughed Anna, as she embraced her parents.

"Is that everyone?" asked George, looking at the readings on his display.

"Yes, George," replied Emma. "And well done, you've done a truly wonderful job today."

"Yes, thanks George," added Harry. "Thank you for trusting us."

"Well," mumbled the old man sheepishly, "I am only human after all."

There followed the introductions of Harry's and Anna's parents to one another, and also of Harry's parents to Anna, and plenty of debating the science of wormholes and the ground-breaking theory surrounding dark matter and the stimulation of black holes.

Eventually, Anna asked what had become of Rience and Sorrel.

"Oh, they weren't a problem," answered Emma. "Thirty seconds in the truth helmet and we had the whole story."

"Truth helmet?" Harry asked suspiciously.

"See what I mean about the Authorities?" Anna muttered cheekily under her breath.

"Okay young lady, that's quite enough," reprimanded her father, glancing somewhat awkwardly at their friend from the Authorities.

Emma smiled shrewdly. "Don't worry, I think I'll let that remark slide, given the situation."

"You've only been back five minutes and you're telling me off already," Anna complained to her parents, quickly adding, "and I love it."

"You'll never be told off by us Harry, whatever you do," said Harry's father, tenderly resting a hand on his son's shoulder.

"So, what were Rience and Sorrel up to anyway?" asked Anna.

"Apparently they were just a couple of typical crooks, out to get whatever they could for themselves," replied Anna's mother. "Only of course, they waited all these years and still failed, thanks to you two."

"How boring," said Anna flatly. "They weren't trying to take over the world or anything like that?"

"Nope, financial gain was all they were after. They wanted to claim the new wormhole technology for themselves, that's all."

"So not all Tamariskians obey the rules all the time?" observed Harry, looking at Emma.

"Apparently not," she replied.

"There's hope for you lot yet?" he declared boldly.

The woman from the Authorities gasped, while the others laughed. "You Earthlings!" she declared. "I'll never understand why we let you through the wormhole, I really won't."

"Speaking of which," said George, with a timely interruption to the conversation. "We have two more visitors on their way?"

"More Authorities people?" enquired Harry nervously.

"No, just a couple of tourists, coming to observe our beautiful Earth sunrise. You have nothing to worry about."

"We're not so bad Harry," Emma said defensively, "once you get to know us."

Harry held back a smirk, as he saw Anna grinning at him, subtly shaking her head and opening her eyes widely in warning.

"Remember, I've only met Rience and Sorrel so far," he said.

"Oh, you have a point there I suppose," admitted Emma.

"Incoming," cried out George. "Clear the area please."

As the travellers from Tamarisk arrived, Anna and her parents moved over next to Harry.

"Are you alright?" Anna asked him thoughtfully.

"Yeah, I'm great," he answered. "What will happen to Rience and Sorrel now?" he queried.

"They'll likely be banished to a prison island near the equator. There's not much there, and it's scorching hot. They won't like it."

Harry considered her answer as the new arrivals, a young man and woman, quickly checked in with George, and looked around with surprise at the busy hub.

"We thought we were the only ones," said the woman to the man. "This is much nicer, they'll be a better atmosphere now."

"What else is there on Tamarisk?" Harry asked Anna. "You haven't told me much beyond what I've seen so far."

"You never asked." Anna laughed.

"And I haven't forgotten your promise to take me to a place with flying cars," he accused.

"That's true," she admitted, "although to be honest, flying cars are overrated anyway. It's a complete nightmare wherever they have them."

"Why's that?"

"Well, imagine if you had them on Earth."

"I have, it would be totally cool."

"Actually it wouldn't, and what would be the point? Think of the noise and total lack of privacy if anyone could fly anywhere. And if you couldn't, but had to follow lanes in the sky, you might as well be on the ground, or under it. Plus you would have to have a pilot's licence to fly anyway, so what's wrong with just having a helicopter? It's not as though flying cars would be any cheaper."

"You know, you can be quite dispiriting sometimes," complained Harry.

"I know," said Anna serenely. "It's just one of my many talents."

Their attention turned back to the couple. "Only one sun," exclaimed the man, putting his arm affectionately around the woman.

"I know, amazing isn't it?" she replied, clutching his waist.

"Are you celebrating a special occasion?" George enquired perceptively.

"We've just got married," the happy couple chorused cheerfully.

"Well, congratulations to you both," said George, as did everyone else in the rather crowded hub. "It's a beautiful autumn day and should be a good sun-up, you've timed it well." He distributed special sunrise glasses to everyone.

"Of course, it's so bright it can make you blind," squealed the woman, jumping up and down excitedly.

"Which reminds me," Harry's mother whispered in his ear from behind him. "Congratulations to you as well. You're going to have a baby brother."

She placed her arms around him and pulled him close.

"Look everybody, here comes the sun," shouted the newly married and enthusiastic man.

As Harry looked fondly at his parents, the spectators stood in contented silence, watching the rising sun creep tentatively from its hiding place beyond the eastern horizon, and the first rays of a glorious new autumnal day fell upon them and the Ring of Stones.

Made in the USA
Charleston, SC
26 April 2016